The Final Temptation

Men of Honor Series

K.C. LYNN

The Final Temptation

Print Edition

Published by K.C. Lynn

Dear reader,

Well, here we are, the last book in the *Men Of Honor* series—Kayla and Cooper's story. I must thank all of you who asked me for their story. I never intended to write one for them, but shortly after *Fighting Temptation* released, and I saw how many of you loved Kayla and Cooper, I knew I would write one. And I am so happy I did. Their story is so different from all the others, but I love it just as fiercely. My other books are filled with suspense and all sorts of heart-wrenching emotions, but I intended for this one to be a light, fun, sexy read. It was a nice change of pace, and I fell even more in love with both Cooper and Kayla.

I have so many feelings as I write this letter to you—excitement, nervousness, and a little sadness—because this was the series that started it all for me. It's the one that brought me such amazing, loyal readers and friends that I know will last a lifetime.

For those of you who have been following me closely you know that even though this is the last book in the *Men Of Honor* series, it is not the last we will be seeing these characters. (Thank goodness, because I'm not ready to let go just yet.) *Acts Of Honor* will be a spin-off series that will consist of five books, Anna and Logan being the first. Feel free to check out my website: www.authorkclynn.com Under *Upcoming Books* you will find out more about this series and what is to come. For teasers and sneak peeks make sure to follow my Facebook page: facebook.com/pages/Author-KC-LYNN/575868539173061

I hope you all love Kayla and Cooper's story as much as me and feel that I did them justice. Thank you for all your love and support. I hope I continue to live up to this pedestal that you have so graciously put me on.

Much Love,
Author K.C. Lynn XO!

Dedication

This book is dedicated to the star herself, my girl Kayla. Kayla, you have been there for me from the beginning and cheered me on to my success. Who knew that when I wrote you into *Fighting Temptation*, and gave you one hot cop boyfriend, that my readers would fall in love with you and request for you to have your own story? Though I am not surprised, you are easy to love. Thank you for always being there for me. The best thing that ever came out of working at Helius was meeting you.

So without further ado, this is for you.

Love you forever.

CHAPTER 1

Kayla

There are certain moments in life that we will remember forever. Some may be a memorable birthday from our childhood, one that stood out a little more than the rest of them; that awkward moment with the first boy you ever kissed; or times with your best friend where you laughed so hard that you cried. Or, in Julia's and my case, times where I got us into deep shit thanks to my dumb ideas and hot temper. And then there were moments that altered the course of your life. They touched you so deeply that every time you think about them, you can still feel what you felt in that moment just as strongly as you did all those years ago.

I'm lucky enough to have a few of those moments, and one of them was the night of my senior prom. Though not because of my success of getting through twelve years of school—nope. It's because it was that night when I found out the one guy, who I had been in love with since I was fourteen years old, returned my feelings. The same one who lived next door to me and tempted my teenage hormones on a regular basis. He's a guy that was born with natural good looks, like insane good looks, like so damn sexy that it should be illegal to look that good. He could charm the panties off any girl who came within reach of him... *Don't think about that part, Kayla.*

He was a natural at sports, good in school, and was loved by everyone—still is. You know that term, *the All-American boy next door*? Well, that was Cooper McKay. But the attributes I just listed are only a very small part of why I fell in love with him. The one thing I love most about Cooper—other than his delectable body of course—is his heart. He is the most honorable and courageous man I've ever known. A man who puts his life on the line every day, and damn does he look good doing it too, uniform and all… *Head out of the gutter, Kayla.*

Okay, in all seriousness, it's his integrity that made me fall madly in love with him. The way he takes care of me and protects me, my friends, and all the other citizens of Sunset Bay. The guy will go to Grams's senior home every time Gladys thinks someone is stealing her panties for crying out loud. Now how many guys do you know that would do that? None, zero, zip, nada—but my Coop will. We all know the real reason why Gladys calls the good sheriff time and time again, and it ain't because she thinks anyone is stealing her panties. She just wants to get a look at the goods, and can you really blame her? I most certainly don't. Though, if she were about forty years younger and looked like Megan Fox, the bitch and I would be having words.

"You look so darn beautiful, Kayla," Grace says softly, breaking into my thoughts.

I smile at her reflection in the mirror as she stands behind me. "Thanks, Grace."

Today I will be adding to those memorable moments in my life, because I am finally going to marry the man I'm madly in love with. Ever since I was a little girl, I dreamed about this day, and I have to admit as I look at my reflection, what I see staring back at me is exactly how I pictured myself. With my white, strapless, poufy dress, high veil, and classy shoes I feel like a modern-day Cinderella. Add along the plantation we chose, which has a beautiful outdoor garden, and of course my very own Prince Charming, it's my dream wedding come true. Although, Cooper is a little more on the rugged side for a prince, but I'll bet good ol' Prince Charming can't do half of the things Coop can with his mouth…

"Miss Gwace is wight. You wook boutiful," Ruthie chimes in, cutting off my perverted thoughts.

With a smile, I turn around and hunch down to her level. "And you look so beautiful too, Ruthie. Thank you for agreeing to be my flower girl, and thank you for parting with your beanie. I know that must have been difficult. But I promise as soon as the ceremony and pictures are finished you can put it right back on."

She gives me a big, gap-toothed grin. "No pwobwem. Da Big Guy and me talked about it and decided it was a small sacwifice to make fwor just one day." All of us bite back a chuckle, knowing how serious her and Cade's beanie obsession is. It's adorable how much she tries to be just like him.

I look around at the beautiful ladies who surround me in this room and feel so blessed. Grace, Katelyn, and Faith all agreed to be my bridesmaids, while Ruthie and Annabelle are my flower girls. And, of course, Julia is my matron of honor. They all look stunning in their pink, silk, strapless dresses, and I know the guys with their pink ties are going to compliment them nicely. I feel my lips tilt with a smirk at the thought. I bet the guys have been grumbling all morning about that, but Coop put up and shut up because it made me happy. One of the other things I love about him so much.

I'm brought out of my thoughts when the bathroom door swings open to reveal a smiling Julia. My heart immediately thrums in anticipation for what she's about to tell me. "So? What does it say?" I ask, but by her expression I already know the answer.

"It's positive," she responds softly.

Silence fills the room as I stare at her. Everyone awaits my reaction, not knowing what to expect. "Positive?" I repeat, making sure I heard her right.

She nods.

I blow out a heavy breath and feel tears blur my eyes but I hold them back, not wanting to ruin my makeup. Walking over, I snatch the pregnancy test from her and stare at the blue plus sign. "Oh my god. Coop and I are going to have a baby," I whisper.

The girls remain quiet, trying to gauge my reaction. Katelyn is finally the one to break the silence. "So, how do you feel about it?"

I think about it for a moment. "I'm really surprised. I didn't think it would happen so soon. I just went off the pill last month, and I heard it usually takes a while for it to leave your system." I pause then look up at them all with a smile. "But I'm really happy."

Everyone rushes over and wraps me in their arms. "Congratulations, Kayla, I'm so happy for both you and Cooper," Faith says, her voice soft and sincere, as always.

A chorus of agreements follow before Grace breaks in. "I can't believe we're gonna have babies together. This is so darn excitin', Kayla." Grace and Sawyer just found out last month that not only are they expecting, but they are also having twins.

"I'm so excited that Annabelle is going to have more play buddies," Julia adds.

"Me, too." I walk over and sit at the end of the bed then stare down at the test, still feeling in utter shock. Although, I guess I shouldn't. I have suspected this the last few days.

"What do you think Cooper will say?" Katelyn asks as she takes the seat next to me.

I feel bad everyone here knows before him, but when I voiced my suspicion to Grace and Julia early this morning they suggested I take a pregnancy test. The need to know one way or another became so overwhelming that I couldn't wait. I didn't want the question on my mind all day.

"I think he will be happy. We talked about not waiting too long, which is why I went off the pill last month, but we also didn't think it would happen this fast." I shrug. "I guess it's meant to be."

"Coop is going to be ecstatic, I know it," Julia says with confidence. "Let's just hope that when you go into labor, he and Jaxson aren't together. Lord knows what would happen after last time."

We both burst out laughing from the memory of the guys being complete lunatics when Julia went into labor with Annabelle. Everyone looks at us in confusion so we fill them in on what happened. I tell them how they both almost drove off without us because they were in such a mad rush, thinking the baby was just going to fall out of Julia at any given second. It isn't long before everyone is laughing just as hard as Julia and me.

"How did you and Mistwer Shewiff meet?" Ruthie asks.

I smile at the memory. "He moved in next door to me when I was fourteen years old. Then it was hook, line, and sinker for that guy."

"Yeah, about three years later and with a little push, or should I say shove, from this girl," Julia says, pointing at me with a giggle.

I shrug but can't suppress my own chuckle. "What can I say, I'm a persistent one when I want something, and that guy didn't stand a chance. Little did I know though, he felt the same way."

"Oh, this sounds like a good story that you must share," Faith says, taking a seat on the other side of the bed, then lifts Ruthie up to sit on her lap.

"Sure, I'd love to share it with you guys."

"It's definitely an entertaining one," Julia adds as she takes her own seat. Grace follows suit and gets comfortable, then everyone waits for me to begin.

"Okay, as I said, Coop moved in next door to me when I was only fourteen. He was seventeen, and let me tell you, he was as sexy then as he is now. The first day I laid eyes on him—it was a sweltering, hot summer day. He was carrying boxes in from the moving truck, with no shirt on, his bronzed skin and toned muscles were flexing with every..."

I trail off and look at Ruthie who watches me with a big smile.

Yeah, I'm going to have to be careful how I word this story.

"Anyway…" I cut my hand through the air and move on. "As I watched him that day, I told myself I was going to marry him. I didn't care what it took, I was going to make it happen." I think about that for a second. "Okay, it sounds kinda creepy right now but remember, I was fourteen at the time."

"You were the same way at seventeen, too," Julia reminds me, her voice laced with amusement.

"This is true," I admit, completely unashamed. "But with Coop, I can't explain it. My crush for him at fourteen was different than it was for any other crush I'd had. Then as the years went on, and I got to know him, my crush turned into love. Unfortunately, he didn't live next door for very long since he moved out with Jaxson after they graduated, but that didn't stop me from trying to see him every chance I could."

Julia giggles and I look at her with a smile as I go back to a time that was frustrating, emotional, and downright beautiful…

I glance at my clock with bleary eyes and realize I'm late. "Shit!" Shooting out of bed with a speed that shocks even myself, I get presentable for school in record time.

I rush into the kitchen and kiss my mom's cheek just before I dash out of the house with an apple in my hand.

"No speeding, Kayla," she yells at me through the window. I wave her off, unconcerned, then send a quick text to Julia, letting her know I'm on my way.

As I get into my vehicle, I notice Cooper's squad car isn't parked outside his parents' house anymore, and I don't know if I'm relieved or disappointed. It's his fault I slept like shit last night. He had my hormones on high alert all damn night.

When I found out he was house-sitting for his parents, while they were on vacation for the next week, I knew it was time to make my move. But no matter how many seductive attempts I've made, the guy hasn't come near me. So last night I pulled out the big guns by prancing around my backyard in the skimpiest bikini I owned. I soaked in the hot tub until my skin was wrinkled to a prune, but the bastard still didn't come over. I know he saw me though; I caught him watching me from his upstairs window, his expression as hard as granite. I'm sure it's because he was just as worked up as me. I see the way he looks at me; I know he wants me just as bad as I want him.

So, why the hell is he holding back and fighting this?

I shake myself from my frustrated thoughts when I pull up to Julia's. She's waiting patiently on the driveway and hops in just as I come to a stop.

"I'm so sorry, I slept in," I apologize, knowing it's a shitty explanation. I hate being late.

Of course, being Julia, she doesn't get mad. "No problem, it happens. I'm hoping you're going to tell me it's because you were up late, making out with Coop." She inquires with a hopeful smile.

I harrumph as I hit the gas and drive a little faster than I should. "No. I wish it were because of that."

"Seriously?" she asks in surprise. "Did you go into the hot tub like we talked about?"

"Yep. I even wore my skimpiest bikini, and the bastard still didn't bite."

She reaches over and touches my arm gently. "I'm sorry, Kayla. If it's any consolation, I know how you feel," she says, referring to Jaxson.

"Yeah, well at least Jaxson still hangs out with you. For the last year it seems all Cooper does is completely avoid me, and I don't understand why. We used to be friends until he dated that bitch Brittany." Just thinking about that whore has anger rushing through my system hot and fast. They dated over a year ago and it still infuriates me to think about. She's probably the biggest bitch I've ever met, and she always made sure to rub Cooper in my face. Thankfully, they only lasted a short month, like most of Coop's relationships over the last few years. It was the happiest day of my life when he broke up with her.

"Well, tonight you could always…" Julia trails off at the sound of police sirens and glances behind us. "Uh-oh."

I look down at my speedometer to see I'm only going seven miles over the legal limit. I growl in frustration and pull over, not happy that we're now going to be even later for school. The cop pulls up behind me, and I stare in complete shock as Cooper steps out of the car.

Are you freaking kidding me?

My stomach does its usual flip as I watch his gorgeous ass make his way over.

Hmmm, maybe this isn't such a bad thing after all.

Getting my wits about me, I roll down my window then stick my head out and give him my best smile. "Well, hey there, Officer Sexy."

With his aviators in place, Cooper stares down at me, his expression unimpressed. "Kayla," he greets in irritation before nodding over at Julia. "How's it going, Julia?"

"Hey, Cooper."

I'm annoyed that his greeting to her is friendlier than mine, but I shrug it off and decide to push his buttons like I always do. Reaching over, I finger his handcuffs at the side of his belt and give him a suggestive smile. "Nice cuffs, Coop. I've always wondered what it would be like to be cuffed to a bed. Maybe you can lock me up sometime."

I hear Julia muffle her laughter, but I don't take my eyes off of him. His expression never wavers, but I know I got to him because his jaw flexes. I love riling him up like this. I'm hoping one day it will finally make him crack and he will let all that frustration loose on me in the dirtiest ways possible.

"License and registration," he says, ignoring my comment.

I tense. "What? Why?"

"Because you were speeding, and I'm going to give you a ticket."

My mouth drops in shock. "You can't be serious."

Now it's his turn to smirk. "I'm very serious."

"Give me a break, Coop, I was going seven over. You have to at least be going ten over to get a ticket."

He stares at me like I'm an idiot. "I can give you a ticket for going one over the legal limit."

I try to gauge his expression, still thinking he can't be serious.

He wouldn't give me a ticket, would he?

No, he wouldn't, he's just screwing with me, I know it. "All right, Officer Romeeooo," I croon, dragging out the name. "Let's be honest here, you really pulled me over because you missed my pretty face this morning. I missed yours too, but this"—I gesture between us—"will have to wait because I'm late for school."

Julia snickers again, but unfortunately Cooper doesn't find it as funny. "You're going to be even later if you don't stop stalling. Give me your license and registration, Kayla. Now."

I gape at him as I realize he's completely serious. With a huff, I pull out my license and registration then hand it to him, knowing I need to get my ass to school. He takes it with a smirk then walks back to his squad car.

I look over at Julia. "I can't believe he's really going to give me a fucking ticket."

She shrugs. "Maybe he's just messing with you to prove a point and he won't actually give you one."

I shake my head, knowing he's going to. He wouldn't do all this then not follow through. Sure enough, he walks back a couple of minutes later and hands me back my license and registration. I don't bother to look at him as I rip them from him. When I go to snatch the ticket out of his hand, his grip tightens on it, not letting go.

My irritation quickly vanishes when he bends down and leans in my window. His delicious, masculine scent penetrates my senses and completely short-circuits my brain. My heart pounds wildly and my breath catches in my throat, as he trails his nose along the side of my cheek until his lips are at my ear. "You need to be careful of the games you keep playing with me and my dick," he whispers, his tone as smooth as whiskey. "Because next time, Kayla, I will not be responsible for my actions, and believe me when I tell you, you are not ready for me, baby. Not yet."

With that, he presses the softest kiss to my cheek and drops the ticket on my lap before strutting his sexy ass away, as if he didn't just completely tilt my world on its axis. I sit stunned for a long moment, wondering if I just imagined his words.

"Whoa." Julia fans herself. "What the heck was that all about?"

She couldn't have heard him, but I'm sure she felt the sexual tension. She had to; it still lingers heavily in the car. I pick up the ticket and see the amount for *one hundred thirty dollars.*

Instead of feeling pissed like I ought to, the biggest smile takes over my face. I think today is going to be a great day after all.

CHAPTER 2

After school lets out, Julia and I grab an ice cream then head over to the ball diamond. "Tell me again why we're coming here?" she asks as we get out of the car.

"Because it's the baseball game of the year—the sheriff's department against the fire department. Sweaty, shirtless hotties with bronzed skin and toned muscles." I shiver just thinking about it. "This is shit we do not want to miss." Although, my eyes will be for one guy only.

My heart rate kicks up in anticipation at getting to see Cooper again. His words have been replaying in my head all day since our run-in earlier.

Next time, Kayla, I will not be responsible for my actions, and believe me when I tell you, you are not ready for me, baby. Not yet.

Oh boy is he wrong. I'm more than ready for his sexy ass. I've had a throbbing between my legs since this morning, hell, for the last three years. He is close to cracking, I can feel it. I just have to figure out what is holding him back.

I used to think it was our age difference; it's almost three years, which is squat in my opinion. He never came right out and said it, but he would make the odd remark about it. I turn eighteen in a few weeks, the day after prom, so there is no way it can be that.

But what the hell is it then?

Julia and I grab a seat up high on the metal bleachers with our ice creams and soak in the incredible view before us. My eyes sift through the shirtless hotties and immediately find the man I came to see, instantly recognizing his body and the tattoo that marks his defined shoulder blade. The American Flag, with the overlying script—*To Serve With Honor*—suits him perfectly. Cooper is the most honorable guy I've ever met. His integrity is what made me fall madly in love with him, and I know he's going to make an incredible sheriff one day.

I watch him tense suddenly then, as if feeling the weight of my stare, he turns around. I can't see his eyes because of his aviators but I feel them as if it were his hands. We watch each other, a long moment stretching between us. He keeps his expression schooled, but it doesn't last long. Giving him a flirtatious smile, I lick my ice cream the same way I want to lick his delectable, hard body.

Even from here I can see his nostrils flare and his jaw flex. I give him a sassy little wave with my fingers, enjoying his torment. He shakes his head in frustration then turns back around, dismissing me.

I look over at Julia and we both laugh. "Lord, girl, one day you're going to push that man too far."

"That's the plan," I tell her truthfully, without feeling an ounce of shame.

"So I heard Matt Greenwood asked you to prom today," she says, quirking an eyebrow in question.

"Yep, but of course I said no. Which probably wasn't a smart idea, considering I haven't been making any headway with you know who." I nod to where Coop is throwing a ball back and forth with another guy from the police department. "I may just end up dateless if I don't think of something soon." The entire thought is depressing. I've thought about just straight out asking Cooper, but I want to be certain of his feelings for me before I do. However, I'm running out of time and I may need to just bite the bullet and do it regardless.

"Well, at least you have been asked. No one has even attempted to ask me," she says sadly. "I don't know why, I mean, I know I'm not a knockout or anything, but I'm a pretty nice girl and I can be a lot of fun to hang out with. Can't I?"

"Of course you are," I tell her truthfully; the girl is full of shit, she's a knockout but she doesn't know it, which only makes her more attractive. "I keep telling you, no one is asking because they're terrified of Jaxson."

"Why would Jaxson care?"

I roll my eyes. I love this girl to death but she is incredibly naïve. "Because he wants you to himself." She shakes her head, dismissing my theory right away. "Yes, he does. I tell you this all the time, Julia. The guy has it bad for you, but he's too fucked up to admit it. Why do you think any guy who has ever remotely tried to ask you out never looks at you again? I'm telling you, Jaxson has laid claim, you just don't know it."

"I wish," she mumbles.

"Trust me, I'm right. Either way, I thought you were going to ask him to go to prom with you?"

"I really want to but I know it's not his thing. He didn't even go to his own prom, so I doubt he would come with me."

I shrug. "You don't know unless you ask."

"Yeah, but I'm a coward. The entire thought of his rejection stings a little too much."

I nod in understanding because I feel the exact same way with Cooper. "Well, if all else fails we can go together?"

She smiles. "I love that idea."

Before we can say more, Mark Stevens climbs up the bleachers and takes a seat between us. *Great!*

"Well hello, ladies," he greets as he throws an arm around each of us, his clothes reeking of marijuana.

"Mark," I acknowledge, before glancing nervously over at Cooper. I see him watching us, his entire demeanor looking downright lethal. *Crap!* I was hoping he wouldn't notice, he hates Mark and I don't want him in a pissy mood after this. Looking away, I bring my attention back to Mark. "What are you doing here? Came to scope out the hotties like the rest of us?"

He grunts. "Fuck that! Like I want to be around a bunch of pigs."

I tense, taking offense to that term. The only reason he doesn't like cops is because he deals with them often over his alleged little side business. The asshole's only savior is his dad, who's a high profile lawyer. Most of the girls in our school play up to him because of his money and status, when in reality he's nothing but an arrogant jerk.

"I'm actually here to meet up with Scott, but since I saw you two beautiful ladies sitting here I decided to personally invite you to this." He hands each of us a printed postcard.

I read it and see it's an invitation to a party this coming weekend in the next town over. "A party in Callingwood?" I ask.

"Yep, and it's not just any party, it's going to be the party of the century. We are combining the graduates of Sunset Bay along with Callingwood and throwing one hell of a farewell party to the life of high school. My buddy's parents own some land buried in the bush, that's where it's being held. There will be kegs, music, a bonfire, and best of all—me." He gestures to himself in arrogance.

I roll my eyes, but have to admit it sounds fun. Well, except for the part that he's going to be there. Suddenly, I feel Mark tense next to me. I glance up to see his face pale as he stares at something ahead. I look over to where his attention is and see Jaxson striding toward us with a look of intent to kill.

"That's my cue, ladies. I'll see you this weekend," he says, then hightails his ass down the back of the bleachers, avoiding trouble altogether.

Jaxson makes his way over, looking pissed.

Yeah right, the asshole hasn't laid claim. Just look at the way Mark hightailed it out of here.

"Hey, Jax," Julia greets him quietly, and moves over for him to sit next to her.

His expression softens marginally. "Hey, Jules." He gives her the usual kiss on her forehead then takes the seat next to her. "Hey, Kayla." He acknowledges me with a nod.

"Hey."

He looks back to Julia. "What the fuck was Mark Stevens doing up here with you guys?"

She shrugs. "He just handed us an invitation for a big, senior class party."

He takes the invitation out of her hand and reads it. "This is in Callingwood," he says, stating something we already know.

"Yep," she replies easily.

"You're not going."

I tense, and Julia falters slightly at his tone. "Excuse me, and why not?"

"Because I don't fucking like that guy. He's bad news."

Julia stares back at him aghast, and I watch her aquamarine eyes flare with irritation. "Well, I'm not going for him. If Kayla and I decide to go it will be because we want to hang out with our graduating class. You do not have a say, Jaxson."

His eyes turn downright lethal. He turns and puts his hands on either side of her hips, caging her in, then leans in close and brings his face only an inch from hers. "Don't push me on this, Julia, I'm serious. I work late that night, and I can't be there to look out for you."

"I don't need a babysitter!" she snaps.

They stare each other down, and I swear you can feel the sexual tension roll off of them in waves.

They seriously just need to get it over with and fuck already.

"Stop being bossy." She pushes against his forehead and moves him out of her personal space.

He relents with a grunt, but we all know this argument is far from over.

Shaking my head, I turn my attention back to the ball diamond. We watch most of the game in silence, except for when I'm cheering my ass off for Cooper, using every kind of pet name I can think of, which ticks him right off. Jaxson chuckles a few times and warns me of the buttons I'm pushing. I just give him a wink, letting him know my intention, and don't let up.

After the game, we make our way down to the chain link fence. My gaze takes in all of Cooper's hot and sweaty, half naked glory as he strides toward us. His shaggy, light brown hair pokes out of the sides of his baseball cap while his long, lean muscles and eight pack are on full display. I get the sudden urge to lick every line and definition, wanting to know if he tastes as good as he looks.

The man is seriously one sexy son of a bitch.

By his expression I can tell he's not happy, probably about my cat-calling him throughout the game. I ignore his brooding demeanor and give him a bright, innocent smile. Then I put one foot in the hole of the chain link and boost myself up. As soon as he reaches us, I lean over and give him a swat on the ass. "Good game, Officer Sexy."

He falters, obviously not expecting the love tap, but keeps his expression schooled. Jaxson and Julia both try to cover their amusement, but one of the guys from his department overhears me and doesn't bother to hide his.

"Officer Sexy." The guy points, proceeding to laugh his ass off.

I start to feel bad about others ribbing him; it's only okay for me to do it, not anyone else. But then I remember the ticket in my car and my guilt fades.

Cooper shoots him a death glare and the guy quickly shuts up, then he brings his attention back at me. My heart pounds wildly as he steps closer, stopping when his face is only a mere inch from mine. Reaching up he takes his aviators off, and I suck in a sharp breath at the intense hunger in his gaze. My smile spreads, knowing my plan is working, but before I can think of anything witty to say he speaks first. "What was Mark Stevens doing with you, and why the fuck were his hands all over you?"

I rear back, not only surprised by his question, but also shocked at how angry he sounds. I know he doesn't like the guy, but I didn't expect him to be this mad.

"He invited them to a bush party out in Callingwood," Jaxson responds before I can.

I glare over at him, not appreciating that he replied to *my* question.

I look back to Coop but once again, before I can get a word in edgewise, he speaks. "You're not going anywhere near there. Do you hear me?"

I tense at the order. "Excuse me?"

"You heard me, Kayla."

Oh, I don't think so.

The only time he can order me around is if he's telling me to shed my clothes. I give him my best glare, not bothering to hide my irritation. "Listen here, buddy, I'm going to tell you the same thing that Julia already told Bossy McBosserson over there," I snap, gesturing behind me to Jaxson. "If we decide to go to that party it's our decision. You have no say."

His eyes turn fierce and his teeth clench until I think his jaw is going to snap. "I know shit about him that you don't. He's not a good guy to be around."

"I wouldn't be hanging out with him. I'd be going to hang out with others from my graduating class."

He shakes his head. "It doesn't matter. Anywhere that guy goes he brings trouble, it's not safe for you."

I soften a little at his concern. "Don't worry, Officer Romeeoo, I can take care of myself." I can tell he's about to argue but I don't give him the chance. "I need to get going, but I'll be in the hot tub again tonight if you want to join me," I inform him with a sassy smile. Then, leaning closer, I whisper, "Except this time I'll give you a better show and take my top off."

A low growl erupts from his chest and the deep, sexy sound of it hits me between the legs.

Being bolder than usual, I turn my face and lay a loud smacking kiss right on his stubbly cheek. Before I end up mauling the poor bastard like I really want to, I force myself to jump down.

I look over at Julia to see her and Jaxson watching us with amusement. I nod at her, signaling it's time to go. She gives Jaxson a hug then follows me. Once we're a little distance away, I turn back around to see Cooper staring at me, his expression holding a promise for retribution, which completely excites me. I blow him a kiss then wink before turning around and heading to my car.

I'm wrapped up in my thoughts, thinking about what my next move will be tonight, when I feel Julia come to an abrupt halt. "Uh-oh," she mumbles nervously.

"What?" I look to where her attention is riveted and my good mood sours quickly when I see Brittany fucking Vail next to my car. She's bent over, looking in my side mirror as she puts on lipstick. The sight of her has fury rushing through me.

Sensing my presence, she looks over at us and gives me a snide smirk.

I'm so not in the mood for her shit today.

The bitch stands and leans against my car, cocking a hip and sticking her fake tits out for the world to notice. I stride toward her easily, trying to calm my angry heartbeat. I hate that she gets to me, and I hate even more to know that Coop has been with her, touched her…

Ugh, don't think about it, Kayla.

"You lost, Brittany? Your street corner is that way." I point off to the left.

She glares at me with the same hatred I feel. "For your information, I'm here to see Cooper, we have plans."

I try to keep my cool because I know she's full of shit. Cooper has nothing to do with her anymore… I don't think.

"But the question is, what are you doing here? Shouldn't you two be at home, getting ready for bed?"

I roll my eyes at her lame insult about our age. She acts like she's ten years older than us rather than two. "Give it a rest, Brittany, and fuck off. Don't you have something better to do than annoy me?"

"Actually, yes, I do. Cooper," she retorts with a smirk, making me want to yank one of her lame pigtails right out of her fucking head.

"You're full of shit. He broke up with you a year ago, and it's time you move on. Clinginess doesn't look good on you, though not much does," I add, taking in her too short top and her barely there skirt.

"Just because we broke up doesn't mean we've stopped fucking."

Her words hit me like a painful blow to the stomach, no matter how hard I try not to let them.

"She's lying. Don't listen to her," Julia whispers next to me.

Brittany releases a snotty laugh. "Oh she wishes, just like I'm sure you wish I never fucked Jaxson."

I feel Julia tense next to me, and my fury spikes to a whole new level now that she's brought her into this. "I'm giving you fair warning, bitch, if you don't get out of my face in the next five seconds, you won't need your circus makeup any longer, because the damage I'll do to you will permanently decorate your face."

She glares back at me, but there is no denying the trepidation in her eyes. She knows I'm serious, and for all of our sakes I hope she listens. With a scoff she pushes off my car and stalks past me, but not before one last blow. "Go home and leave the guys for the girls who know what to do with them."

I clench my fists and restrain myself from turning around to watch her retreating back, knowing if I do I will tackle the bitch. I stand frozen for a long second and stare at my car, hating the sick feeling that's plaguing me right now.

"What a lying slut," Julia seethes. When I don't respond, and remain still, she touches my arm gently. "She's lying, Kayla, I know it."

I nod and give her a small smile, though not a convincing one. I want to believe Cooper would have nothing to do with her, but why else would she have come here?

We both get into the car, and as soon as I close my door, something on my side mirror catches my attention. "Ugh, that bitch!" I growl, staring at the bright red lipstick on my mirror that spells out *SLUT*.

"Are you serious?" Julia asks, aghast. "She has some nerve!"

I rip some tissue out of my purse and try wiping it off, but it only smears and makes a mess. I give up and toss the garbage in my backseat, then make the mistake of looking toward the ball diamond to see the whore rubbing herself all over Cooper. I quickly look away, because the pain lancing me is heart-stopping.

"If you want to change your mind about taking the bitch out, I got your back," Julia offers, trying to lighten the mood.

I release a slight chuckle and look over at her. One of the best things that happened to me was her moving here two years ago. We always have each other's back, and even though she could never hurt a fly, I know she would swing her fists and try her best just for me. I'd love nothing more than to kick Brittany's ass, but the charges wouldn't be worth it. I have to tread carefully; my dad's trying to get her dad as a client. But the bitch needs to be taught a lesson… Suddenly, an idea forms, and it's a really good one. I give Julia a mischievous smile.

"Uh-oh, why are you smiling like that?" she asks nervously.

"Be ready late tonight and dress in dark clothes."

"Why, what are we doing?"

I feel my smile spread. "We're going to get even."

CHAPTER 3

I decided to have Julia meet me at the park late that night, knowing it wouldn't be smart for either of us to have our cars for this.

At five after eleven she comes jogging down the dark path that's marginally lit up by the houses on either side. She's out of breath by the time she reaches me. "Okay, I'm here. Sorry I'm late, I was with Jax."

"It's all right. It's better that we're later anyway. Come on."

We start walking toward Brittany's house and she eyes the bag in my hand with curiosity. "What's in there?"

"Our props." When I feel her continue to stare at me with questions, I give her a few more details. "We're going to fuck with her car like she did mine."

She stops abruptly. "Oh, Kayla, I don't think this is a good idea. I hate her as much as you, but what happens if we get caught?"

"We won't. Her place is massive so her neighbors aren't that close."

She eyes me hesitantly.

"Look, someone needs to teach this bitch a lesson and I'm going to do it. You don't have to come if you don't want to. I will completely understand. Or you can just stand and keep watch."

She blows out a breath. "No, of course I'm coming with you. I'm just scared of getting caught. Jax will kill me."

I roll my eyes. "Well, tell the guy he has no say in your life unless he's fucking you."

Her cheeks turn pink and she bites her lip. "Do you think he finally would if I said that?"

We stare at each other for a long moment then burst into a fit of laughter and start walking again. "He will come around one day. I know he cares about you, you can see it every time he looks at you."

She shrugs and I know it's because she doesn't believe me. "I talked to him about what happened with Brittany earlier," she starts quietly. "We were right, she lied. He never slept with her and he was pissed when I told him what she said to us. He also said, as far as he knows, Cooper hasn't had anything to do with her since they broke up."

As glad as I am to hear that I'd rather hear it from Cooper, to know it's the truth. "I hope that's the case, because if not, Julia, then I will have to make the decision to give up and move on. It was hard enough on me when he dated her, but if he's been screwing her for the last year, after knowing my feelings for him…" I shake my head, unable to say it. I can't even think it.

She links her arm with mine to offer comfort and we walk the rest of the way in silence. A few minutes later we turn down the street with big, fancy houses, and I'm thankful to see Brittany's lame, pink BMW is parked on her driveway and not in her garage.

"Come on." I start jogging, pulling Julia with me.

"Oh god, oh god, I'm so scared for this," she whispers, trying to keep up.

I roll my eyes at what a worrywart she is. "Would you stop worrying? We will do this quick—it will be done and over with before you know it."

I get down on my knees next to the driver's side door and Julia follows suit. "Okay, what are we doing?"

I hand her the jar of peanut butter and a knife. "Put this under the handle of her door."

With a giggle she takes the peanut butter and does what I say.

Next, I reach in and grab a baggie filled with small rocks I gathered earlier, and proceed to put them into the small holes of her hubcaps.

"What does that do?" she asks, moving closer to me.

"It makes a bunch of racket and sounds like her tires are about to fall off." I shrug. "I did some research in a quick amount of time."

"It won't cause an accident, will it?"

"No, of course not. I want to teach the bitch a lesson, not kill her, or more importantly, someone else."

She nods. "I didn't think so, but just wanted to double-check."

We both giggle then after we finish with the rocks, I reach in and pull out a pair of rubber gloves and a brown paper bag. "You might want to hold your breath for this," I warn her as I put the gloves on.

"Why, what's in it?"

"Dog shit," I reply, barely containing my laugh.

"What? How on earth did you get dog poop? You don't even own a dog."

"A neighbor a few houses down from me has one. It was a nasty task, but it will be worth it." Holding my breath, I open the bag then put my hand on the bottom of it and turn it inside out, using it as a tool to smear the shit all over the side of her car.

"Oh god, that smells so bad." Julia pinches her nose with a chuckle and backs up.

I finish quickly since I'm about to pass out from lack of oxygen, then throw the paper bag along with the nasty gloves back into the plastic bag and tie it in a knot. Glancing around, I quickly run and throw it in their garbage can, making sure to shuffle the trash around so it's buried. I don't breathe again until I have my sanitizer out and am dousing my hands in it.

"Okay, is that it? Can we go now?" Julia asks hopefully.

"No, one last thing." Reaching into my purse, I pull out two black markers and hand one to her. She looks at it curiously then follows me as I walk to the back of her car. Across the rear of the trunk I write, *penis swallower*, knowing everyone who drives behind her will see it.

"Oh my god." Julia covers her mouth in horror but can't contain her snicker.

"What? It's not permanent, it will wash off, just hopefully not before others see it." I nod at her hand. "Write something for what she said about Jax. Believe me, it will make you feel better."

With a grin plastered on her face she writes, *I'm as fake as my boobs.*

I burst out laughing. "Good one."

"Thanks, and you're right, I do feel better."

We begin to laugh uncontrollably, and are so caught up in our amusement that we don't hear anyone come up behind us until it's too late. "What the fuck do you guys think you're doing?"

A startled scream rips from us both as we flip around and land painfully on our butts. As soon as I get my wits about me, I quickly slap a hand over Julia's mouth, since she's still screaming, and look up at a very pissed off Cooper.

Oh shit!

I stare at him, wondering how I should start.

He shifts his focus to the writing behind us then leans to the side and looks at the dog shit smeared on her car. "You have got to be fucking kidding me." He expels a laugh that doesn't sound funny at all and shakes his head.

"Coop, I can explain."

"Not here!" he snaps and hauls us both up by our arms. "Get into my fucking car before anyone else sees you guys."

He starts to drag us toward his squad car, that's parked across the street, but I dig my heels in. "Wait." I rip out of his grasp then run back a couple of steps to pick up my pens. "Uh, don't want to leave any evidence behind." I hold up the markers briefly before putting them in my purse.

Julia tries to bite back her chuckle but fails miserably. Unfortunately, Cooper doesn't find anything funny about it. I swear, if steam could blow out of his ears right now it would. I get my ass in gear and link arms with Julia as we make our way to his car. I take notice that his lights are off, probably to make sure we wouldn't know he was coming.

The tricky bastard.

"You don't think he's going to arrest us, do you?" Julia whispers, seeming terrified at the thought. I shake my head. He wouldn't do that...I don't think.

He opens the back door for us and Julia crawls in first. I think about asking if I can sit up front with him, but with one look at his expression, I decide against it and follow in behind her. We both jump when he slams the door.

"Oh man, we are in so much trouble," Julia whispers shakily.

"I got this. Just play it cool."

Cooper slams his door as he gets in. As he pulls away, he wastes no time laying into us. "What the fuck do you girls think you're doing?"

"Okay, now just calm down, I can explain."

He falls silent, and I try to think of where to start but have a hard time finding words. "I'm waiting!" he snaps.

I clear my throat. "Well, for starters, the bitch deserved it."

A bitter laugh escapes him. "Well that just clears it right the fuck up, doesn't it?"

I glare at him, not appreciating his attitude.

"And you?" He gestures to Julia. "I thought you were with Jaxson tonight. Does he know about this? I'm going to assume not or else he would have stopped you."

Julia tenses, the comment clearly pissing her off, like it does me. "Jaxson has no say in what I do unless he's fucking me," she snaps.

I give her a proud punch in the arm for telling him like it is and she nods in return.

Cooper sees our exchange in the rearview mirror and shakes his head. "Jesus, do you girls even realize that you just committed a fucking crime?"

"Oh give me a break, Coop, it's not like we cut her brakes, for god's sake. All we did is smear some dog shit and peanut butter on her car."

"And the marker, don't forget the marker," Julia whispers, which has us both bursting into a fit of giggles at a really bad time.

"I'm glad you girls are finding this shit so funny." I roll my eyes, but before I can say anything, he whips out his phone and calls someone. "I'm bringing Julia by so you can drive her home," he says, to who I'm assuming is Jaxson.

"Uh-oh," Julia whispers nervously.

"I'll let her tell you the fucking story… Yeah, we're almost there."

After he hangs up I let him have it. "You didn't need to bring Jaxson into this. It's none of his business."

His angry eyes snap to mine in the rearview mirror. "Would you rather I drive her home myself so Margaret can ask why she's in the back of my cop car?"

Good point, but I don't bother to voice that.

We pull up to Jax and Coop's apartment building just a short two minutes later and see a concerned Jaxson waiting outside. I reach over and grab Julia's hand when Coop gets out of the car. "Stay strong, don't take no shit. The bitch deserved it."

She nods then we both step out of the car as Cooper opens the back door.

"Jules, what's going on?" Jaxson asks, rushing over to her. "I thought you said you were going home to bed?"

"Well—I—um—I," she stammers then blows out a breath. "I lied because I had plans with Kayla that I couldn't tell you about. I'm sorry." Her voice is soft and drips with guilt.

"What do you mean you fucking lied?" he asks, clearly pissed.

"Just like she said. She lied because she couldn't tell you. Now back off!"

He rears back at my outburst but I've had enough of both him and Cooper.

The bossy assholes.

"Stay out of it, Kayla, and get back in the car," Cooper orders.

My fists clench at my sides, and I'm just about to tell him where he can go but Julia ends up stopping me by pulling me into a hug. "Go. I'll be okay, I promise. I'll text you later."

My anger evaporates, and I hug her back tightly. "I'm sorry we got busted. I'll take the heat if it comes down to it," I whisper, feeling like shit since she didn't want to do it in the first place and it was my idea.

"No. No matter what happens we're in this together. But I'm sure it will work out."

I nod, but don't feel very confident with how mad Cooper is.

I get back in the car but this time in the passenger side. No way am I going in the back again. Angry silence weighs heavily in the car when Cooper pulls away. He doesn't look over at me once; he stares straight ahead and completely ignores me.

"Don't you think you're overreacting just a little bit, Cooper? It was fucking peanut butter and dog shit."

"It doesn't matter. It's still vandalism, Kayla, what part of that do you not understand?"

"The bitch needed to be taught a lesson!"

He shakes his head as if I'm being ridiculous.

"You know, it's really nice how fast you jump to her defense and blame everything on me." Hurt starts creeping in, mixing with my anger.

He throws his hands up. "What the hell are you talking about? I caught you red-handed committing a crime, how the fuck is it not your fault?"

"She fucked with my car first!"

"Then report it. Don't act like an immature adolescent!"

I grind my teeth, his comment taking my anger to a whole new level. "Of course you're taking her side. I guess I shouldn't be surprised since you're still fucking her."

He tenses, clearly caught off guard by my statement. "What did you just say?" he asks, his tone deadly calm.

"You heard me." Now that I think about it, it makes sense. Why else would he be there? "Did I ruin your booty call for you, Cooper? Is that what you're so pissed off about?" Just the thought has me feeling sick to my stomach.

"Watch it, Kayla, you don't know what the fuck you're talking about."

"No? I had a nice little visit from her today after your game. She waited by my car just to tell me how you guys are still screwing. Of course, that was after she wrote *slut* on my side mirror with her lipstick."

Out of the corner of my eye, I see his grip tighten on the steering wheel, but I don't look over at him—too afraid of what I will see. Is he mad because it's a lie, or is he mad because I found out? I think about the way she hung on him today at the ball diamond and how he didn't push her away.

His silence is all the confirmation I need, and the pain that slices through me is so intense it hurts. I try to hold on to my composure, not wanting him to know how much he has hurt me.

I'm thankful when we finally pull up into his parents' driveway a minute later. I bolt out of the car and quickly rush over to my house, not wanting to be around him for another second, but he intercepts me by grabbing my arm. "Whoa, hold up, baby, we are nowhere near fucking done here."

His 'baby' has me losing all control. I rip out of his grasp and spin around. "What?" I spread my arms out wide. "You gonna arrest me, Cooper? Over fucking peanut butter and dog shit!"

"Would you stop shouting and listen to me for a goddamn minute?" he snaps under his breath.

"No! I don't want to hear any more. You can go fuck yourself!" I turn back around and start off again but I don't make it far.

With a low growl he grabs me from behind, then picks me up and hauls me toward his house.

"What are you doing? Let go of me!" I kick and fight, needing to be away from him. I'm so close to losing it; I can feel tears flooding my eyes, and I don't know how much longer I can keep them from falling. He plows through his back door, almost knocking the thing off its hinges, then hauls me into his kitchen. "I mean it, Cooper, let go of me." I fight harder, even more desperate for escape when I feel hot tears slipping down my cheeks.

"No, you are not going anywhere until you fucking hear me out!" He spins me around, his expression fierce, but it immediately softens when he sees my tears. "Jesus, Kayla, I'm not fucking her."

"Don't lie!" I grind out through the burning ache in my throat. "I saw her hanging all over you after the game."

"Then you didn't look for very long or you would have seen me push her away! I've had nothing to do with her since I broke up with her and I don't want to. I haven't fucked anyone in the last year because some pain in the ass blonde has been consuming my every fucking thought!"

I gape at him, almost certain that he's talking about me. At least he better be, or the other blonde pain in the ass is going to be hearing from me.

We stare at each other for a long moment, the air thick with tension. His hands still grip my arms tightly when something passes between us, something powerful.

"You know what? Fuck it!" Then suddenly it happens, the one thing I have been wanting from him for three long years. He kisses me, his mouth crashing to mine—hard, hot, and demanding.

Oh god.

My knees go weak and a whimper escapes me at the first sweep of his tongue. His taste—his incredible, masculine taste—floods my senses and sets my body on fire. I waste no time giving just as good as I get. My fingers weave into his hair with a grip that draws a growl from him, and I match him stroke for every desperate stroke, taking what I have ached for, what I have dreamed about for so long.

Catching me off guard, he picks me up by my ass and walks us a few steps. I hear a bunch of shit crash to the floor before my back suddenly meets the cold, hard surface of his kitchen table. We never break the kiss, our mouths devouring one another, our tongues dueling a beautiful battle of frustration and pure, hot lust. My lungs crave oxygen but I can't stop, I don't want to, I need more. I rip open his uniform shirt and the tiny buttons fly all over the place. My hands slip beneath his undershirt and roam over the smooth, hard plains of his abs.

With a groan he rips his mouth from mine, and starts trailing his lips down my throat. "You drive me fucking crazy!" he growls. "The way you torment my dick, prancing around this tight, little body of yours. Testing every measure of my control."

And I finally snapped it. Thank the Lord!

Before I can put that thought into words, he rips the top of my tank top down and immediately frees my breasts from the pink lace confines of my bra.

"Look how pretty your tits are," he croons, his dirty words intensifying the throbbing between my legs. "Even fucking better than I imagined."

I'm so drunk with desire that I can't form a coherent word, let alone a witty reply. Cupping the swollen, achy mounds, he leans in and takes a tortured bud between his warm, firm lips.

"Oh god, yes." I arch into his mouth as the most amazing sensations flow through me. His teeth graze my sensitive tip while his fingers work my other, pinching with a force that has my pussy clenching with an intensity that hurts. Lifting my hips, I grind against his erection and whimper when I feel how hard he is. "Cooper, please," I beg with a whimper. "I ache so bad."

Growling, he reaches down and cups me through my yoga pants. "Oh yeah? Has this sweet little pussy been wet and aching for me, baby?"

His words send another wave of heat to soar through me. "Yes. So bad, and for so long," I confess on a moan.

"Good!" he snaps. "Because that's what you do to me. You've been torturing my dick for years with that smart mouth of yours."

I falter, his words bringing joy to explode through my chest. Okay, so it isn't *I love you* but at least I know he has been wanting me as bad as I've been wanting him.

"Well then, what are we waiting for?" I reach for his pants, ready to get this show on the road, but he stops my attempt with a growl and locks my arms above my head.

"No! The only one who will be doing the touching tonight is me." I scoff at that and go to reach for him again, but his grip tightens on my wrists and his jaw clenches in restraint. "I mean it, Kayla. Only me, or everything stops now."

I stare at him and quickly realize he's serious. I'm about to argue but he doesn't give me the chance. Leaning down, he takes a nipple into his mouth again while his hand slips into my pants and his fingers glide through my wet flesh. A fiery whimper escapes me as he skims over my swollen clit, just before he thrusts two fingers inside of me. I gasp and arch at the sweet invasion.

"Ah yeah," he groans. "As tight as I knew you would be. That's because no one else has been here. Right, baby?" I nod in response because I'm too lost in my desire to speak. "That's right. Because this is fucking mine!"

"Yes," I moan breathlessly. Little does he know, I'm all his—body and soul—but I decide to keep that to myself for now. The man already has enough power over me, and quite frankly it's a little scary.

"Do you have any idea what you've been doing to me these last few days? Hell, the last few years. Watching you in that fucking hot tub last night, having to jack off for any relief so I didn't come down there and bend you over the side of it, and fuck you from behind like the animal you're making me."

Oh god.

The image in my head, along with the pleasure of his fingers, has my body feeling like it's about to combust. I try to wiggle closer to him, wanting so desperately to touch him, but he won't release my wrists.

"Cooper, please," I plead. "I want to touch you, too."

He smirks down at me. "You wanted to know what it feels like to be cuffed, baby. Isn't that what you said?"

Oh, he does not want to play this game with me, because I will play right back. I try to clear the fog of arousal clouding my head. "Yes, but that's in your bed when you are fucking me with your cock, not your fingers."

His heavy-lidded eyes turn wild as he expels a mumbled chuckle. "You and that sassy fucking mouth of yours. Soon, Kayla. Soon you will find out what I'm going to do to it, and you will learn quickly just who's in charge here. During the day you can run your mouth all you want, but when your clothes are off and my cock is inside of you, that's my territory, baby."

Holy hell he can be sexy when he's arrogant, but as much as I love his demand right now, I want something more from him. I need it to be more. "If you won't let me touch you, will you at least kiss me?" I whisper, hoping I don't sound as vulnerable as I feel.

His expression softens just before he leans down and gives me his mouth. Our tongues intertwine again, but this time the pace is slower and more intimate, giving me the connection I crave. He finally releases my wrists and allows me to wrap my arms around his neck. I decide not to push my luck, not wanting him to stop me from holding him close.

I gasp when his fingers speed up their delicious assault, stroking a part inside of me I never knew existed. Moaning into the kiss, I hook my legs around his lower back to bring him closer. My hips start rocking to the rhythm of his hand with desperation as I feel myself teeter on the edge.

His growl vibrates against my lips. "That a girl, I can feel how close you are, Kayla, give it to me, let me feel it all over my hand, baby." As soon as he mumbles the words, his free hand cups the soft weight of my breast and his fingers pinch my sensitive nipple with a force that sends me crashing over the edge.

White lights explode behind my eyes and ecstasy rushes through every vein in my body, stealing the breath from my lungs. Cooper swallows my cries of release until every last ounce of pleasure spills from my body.

As I float down from my high and back to reality, I feel him remove his hand quickly. Before he can pull away, I tighten my hold on his neck and kiss him for all I'm worth, not wanting this connection with him to end, but unfortunately, it does, and all too soon.

With a groan, he reaches up and forcibly unlinks my hold from around his neck then walks to the other side of the kitchen. He braces his arms on the counter, keeping his back to me, and drops his head in defeat.

"Cooper, what is it?" I ask, confused at his sudden turmoil. His silence has a sick feeling forming in the pit of my stomach. I quickly put my bra back in place and right my shirt before hopping off the table. I walk toward him slowly, then lay my hand tentatively on his heaving back and feel him tense. "What? Did I do something wrong?" My question drips with insecurity, which bothers me because I am not an insecure person.

"Jesus, no," he breathes out before spinning around and pulling me against him. I feel his erection against my stomach and his body wound tight. I wrap my arms around his waist and soak in his warmth. "Kayla, as much as I want you to stay right now, baby, I need you to leave."

At the restraint in his tone, I look up at him and suck in a sharp breath at his tortured expression. Without hesitation, I reach up and cup the side of his face. "Coop, talk to me."

He watches me for a moment, his jaw flexed and his eyes ablaze. "I'm barely holding on to my control right now." Every word he breathes is through clenched teeth. "If I fuck up here I could lose my job. Do you understand?"

I do now. It finally dawns on me—it's because I'm underage, that's what's been holding him back. Even though I am only weeks away from my eighteenth birthday that doesn't matter to Cooper. His oath to uphold the law weighs heavily on him, and I've been tormenting him to break that oath without realizing it.

"I'm sorry," I whisper guiltily. "I wasn't thinking."

He shakes his head, seeming like he wants to say something but holds back. Instead, he leans down and presses a hard kiss to my forehead. He turns to walk away but I grab his shirt before he can escape and stare up at him.

My heart pounds in my chest for what I'm about to ask but I feel like it's now or never. "Come to prom with me." His eyes widen in surprise, but before he can answer I slap my hand over his mouth. "Don't answer yet, just think about it. Please." I pause and lick my lips nervously. "I've turned down a lot of offers, Cooper, because I want you to take me. I don't want to go with anyone else. I understand your reasoning for all of this now." I gesture between us. "And I don't expect anything from you but to be my date. Although, I will remind you that I turn eighteen at midnight that night, so…" I trail off with a smirk.

Removing my hand, I reach up on my tiptoes and kiss his jaw before slipping past him. Just as I make it to his door, he calls out to me. I stop and look back at him.

"Promise me you won't go to that party this weekend."

"Coop…" I breathe out and shake my head, not understanding why he's being so stubborn about this.

"Please, Kayla."

It's easy to see how concerned he is about it, and since it really isn't a huge deal to me if I go, I relent with a nod. "Okay. I promise."

Walking out the door, I make my way across the driveway to my house. Just as I'm about to walk in, I feel his eyes on me, and turn to see him watching me from his back door, making sure I get in safely. With a smile, I blow him a kiss and don't miss his small smirk in return.

After a hot shower I get settled into bed, my body feeling the most satisfied it ever has, but unfortunately, my heart does not, and I know it won't until I finally have all of Cooper, body and soul.

CHAPTER 4

Saturday morning I walk down the stairs to see my mom and dad sitting at the kitchen table eating breakfast.

"Hi, honey, have a seat. I made pancakes," my mom says, immediately dishing me a plate.

As I take the chair next to my dad, he leans over and kisses my cheek. "Morning. How's my girl?"

I smile and return his kiss. "Good. You aren't working this weekend? Should I have a heart attack?"

I love my father, but he's a workaholic. It's rare to see him on a Saturday morning but I know it comes with owning your own business. He runs the best construction company around, and I'm really proud of him for all of his success.

"Ha, ha," he replies with an amused smirk. I get my smart-ass attitude from him so he knows I'm just messin' with him. "Actually, I took the day off since I have a meeting tonight." He pauses, suddenly seeming uncomfortable. "I'm having a prospective client and his family over for supper. I'm hoping you will be around to join us?"

I shrug. "Sure. Who is it? Do I know them?" I'm assuming I do since everyone knows everyone in this town.

I can tell by my parents' expressions that I'm not going to like this. "Yes, actually, you do. It's the Vails."

"What?" I shout in outrage. "No, Dad! No way is that bitch sitting at my kitchen table."

"Kayla, language," my mom scolds, but I ignore her.

"How could you invite them here for supper? You know how much I hate Brittany."

My dad's expression turns remorseful. "It was her father who suggested it. He thought our families could get to know each other while we talked business."

"Hell no! I already know her, and like I said, she's a class A bitch."

My mom cuts in now. "Honey, why don't you give her a chance? Who knows, it might surprise you and y'all could end up becoming really good friends."

I roll my eyes at how delusional she can be. "Trust me, I will never, ever be friends with her."

"She can't be that horrible if Cooper dated her."

I stiffen and feel as if someone just kicked me in the stomach. My teeth grind, and I try to remember that my mom doesn't know about my feelings for Cooper. I haven't purposely kept it from them; I just haven't exactly found the right time to bring it up. Although, I am a little surprised they haven't caught on.

I shake my head vehemently, not wanting to see that bitch ever again, let alone in my own house.

My father reaches over and puts his hand gently on my arm. "Can you please put aside your differences for tonight? This will be a huge contract for my company if I get it, Kayla. It would be years of work for us. Please, honey, can you do this for me?"

I stare into my dad's pleading blue eyes, which are the same color as mine, and feel my resolve slipping. He's wanted the contracts on the Vail's malls for so long. He's given me so much and has worked hard to make sure my mom and I could have everything we've ever needed. No matter how much I want to, I can't say no to him.

"Fine," I relent on a sigh. "But I'm not staying long, Dad, I will only be able to put up with her for so long. Also, I have plans with Julia, so if it's all right I'm going to invite her, too."

He nods and gives me a relieved smile. “Yes, of course. She’s always welcome here, and I promise just a couple of hours then you can go.” Leaning over, he kisses my cheek again. “Thank you, sweetheart.”

Yeah, well, he better not thank me yet. I just pray I can bite my tongue long enough to get through this. I suddenly think about what I did to her car the other night and realize this could get very ugly.

Yep, just like I expected, a giant clusterfuck. Right when I thought there was no way this night could get any worse, I was wrong. Because my mom ended up inviting Cooper over at the last minute to join us, thinking it would be nice for him to have a home-cooked meal since he will be going back to his apartment soon. He was completely caught off guard when he walked in to see the Vails. But Brittany? Oh, the bitch was overjoyed, and before I could take the seat next to him, she did, which left Julia and me to sit directly across from them. To say you can cut the tension with a knife is a huge understatement.

I watch her sidle up close to the man I have been in love with for three years, the same one who gave me the best orgasm of my life just the other night. My heart pounds in fury and my body vibrates with the urge to punch her out when she leans over and whispers suggestively in his ear with a giggle. Even though it’s apparent that Cooper is uncomfortable with how she’s acting, he doesn’t push her away. I assume he doesn’t want to cause a scene, but regardless, it pisses me right off. I glare at him, not bothering to hide my irritation, and feel Julia put her hand on my bouncing knee in comfort; I’m sure she can tell I’m about ready to commit murder.

Small talk happens amongst the parents, but I do nothing except shovel heap loads of food in my mouth, hoping it will keep me quiet long enough to get through this disaster and not ruin the night for my dad. But I’m finding it very difficult when all I keep hearing is that bitch giggling. I don't bother to glance up, not wanting to know what she's giggling about.

"Did James tell you Brittany's car was vandalized the other night?" Mrs. Vail asks my parents.

Julia and I both tense and my mother gasps in horror. "Oh my gosh. No, he didn't, that's horrible."

"What did they do to it?" my father asks.

Mrs. Vail clears her throat, and I take a sip of my drink, suddenly needing to wash down the thickness in my throat. "They wrote obscene messages on the trunk of her car and spread feces on it."

I should have never taken that drink, because, before I can stop myself, I choke on the smooth liquid. I slap a hand over my mouth, trying to cover the laugh bubbling up from my throat. Julia pats me on the back, and I can tell she's having a hard time containing herself, too.

"Honey, are you all right?" my mom asks in concern, completely oblivious.

I finally manage to pull myself together. "Yes, sorry, it just caught me off guard," I mumble then glance at Brittany to see her glaring at Julia and me. I bite back a smirk and just can't refrain myself from saying, "That really is awful. Why do you think someone would do that to you?"

"I have no idea," she grinds out. "But I know Coop will find out who did it and make them pay. Won't you, baby?" she croons, leaning closer to him.

My amusement vanishes and my fists clench under the table with the need to punch her smug face that's decorated with clown makeup, like usual. I quirk a brow at Cooper and wait for him to say or do something. He shifts in his seat but I'm not sure if it's to move away from her or because he's uncomfortable. Either way, the fact that he isn't outright pushing her away has my anger reaching a whole new level.

"Well, I'm glad nothing too serious was done and she wasn't injured," my father says, trying to break the awkward tension that has settled over the table once again.

Mr. Vail nods. "Yes, us too, and we feel very confident with Cooper's ability to catch the hooligans who did this."

Even though I'm incredibly pissed off right now at Cooper, I still can't help but feel guilty for the position he's in.

"So, Kayla, what are your plans after graduation?" Mrs. Vail asks, changing the subject. "What college are you attending?"

I take a deep breath and try to calm the storm of conflicting emotions swirling inside of me. "Actually, I'm not going to college. I plan to take the massage therapy program at the health and wellness center in Charleston in the fall."

"You want to be a massage therapist?" she asks, as if not understanding that concept.

I try to be as polite as I can and not show my irritation. "Yes, ma'am, I'm also planning to practice Chinese medicine and do acupuncture."

"Oh, well... That's nice, dear." I don't look up from my plate, suddenly feeling uncomfortable, like my choice to not go to some Ivy League college makes me inferior.

"Yes, very nice," Brittany adds snidely, which has my heart rate thumping madly again.

"I think it's something you will be really good at."

My head snaps up in surprise at Cooper's words and my heart warms. I also get a small level of satisfaction at the jealousy on Brittany's expression.

"I agree," my mother says, cutting in. "This is something Kayla has always been passionate about. Ever since she was a little girl, she has always wanted to help people. She will be graduating with honors and we are very proud of her."

I look over at my mother and smile, her words meaning a lot to me in this moment.

"Well, that's great." Mr. Vail joins in on the conversation now. "And you know, there isn't a massage therapy clinic here in Sunset Bay, so you could even open your own business if you wanted."

"That's my plan one day," I tell him truthfully. "And I know just the man to build it for me." I look over at my father with a smile and he winks at me.

"And what about you, dear?" Mrs. Vail asks Julia.

"Oh—well," Julia stammers nervously, never liking to be the center of attention. "I'm hoping I get accepted to the University of Charleston. I want to get my teaching degree."

"A teacher?"

Julia nods. "Yes, I would love to teach elementary school one day like my mother did."

"And you will be the best teacher any kid can have," I chime in, slinging an arm over her shoulder.

She smiles back at me. "Thanks."

"How about you, Brittany?" my mom asks. "Your mother said you are attending the University of Charleston. What is your major?"

"Business," she boasts proudly in her usual annoying voice. "I plan to start my own company as well, though not anything like Kayla. My plan is to open a high-end, successful fashion boutique."

I don't miss her not-so-subtle hint, and before I can stop myself, I snort. The only business that girl could run successfully is a whore-house.

The room falls silent again, and I feel Brittany's glare on me.

Oops.

"I was actually just telling Cooper all about my plans last night over supper, and he liked my ideas."

I falter at her words and feel like I've just been slapped in the face.

My eyes snap to Cooper, and I see his head fall back in defeat, looking rather upset that he's been busted. The bastard lied to me. Something I didn't think he would ever do.

"Wow, two nights in a row for supper together?" I ask, trying to keep the hurt and anger out of my tone, but know I don't succeed.

He is about to say something but Mrs. Vail cuts him off. "Oh yes, Cooper is at our house often for supper, and we always enjoy having him."

I try to rein in the pain and fury rushing through me right now, but my control finally snaps when Brittany leans over and kisses his cheek. "I hope you're still coming to the lake house with us next weekend."

Okay, that's fucking it.

I lean over, pretending to reach for the butter, and knock her full glass of red wine over, making sure it spills on both of them, which isn't hard since she's practically on top of him. Brittany gasps and flies backward.

"Oops. Sorry 'bout that," I deadpan, clearly not meaning it.

"Uh-oh," Julia mumbles.

"You bitch, you ruined my brand new Vera Wang top."

"Brittany!" her father scolds.

The room erupts in chaos as everyone rushes to Brittany's aid. I feel Cooper's eyes on me but I don't look at him, I can't, and I can't look at my father either.

"Come on." I grab Julia's hand, needing to get the hell out of here. "I'm sorry, Dad," I whisper as I rush past him.

"Kayla, where are you going?" my mom calls out, but I don't stop and answer her, my throat getting tighter by the second.

Julia swipes her purse from the couch as we make our way to the door. I decide to forgo mine, not wanting to run to my room to get it. Once we're outside, I tug Julia behind me, urging her to move faster to my car.

"Kayla, wait! Get back here!" Cooper shouts as he chases after us, but again, I don't stop. I get in and immediately start the car, then as soon as Julia's ass hits her seat, I'm peeling out of my driveway. "Fuck!" I faintly hear his curse through my open window as I speed down the street.

It isn't until I'm far enough away that I finally take a deep breath, though it's a struggle through the lump that's lodged in my throat.

"Well, that was intense," Julia whispers, trying to find words for the clusterfuck we just left behind. I don't say anything, I stare straight ahead, the road blurring in front of me from the tears clouding my eyes. She reaches over and places a hand on my leg. "Are you okay?"

I shake my head, because I'm not. I'm angry, hurt, confused, and most of all, I feel guilty for just ruining everything for my father.

"She was just doing it to hurt you, Kayla. Don't let her win. It was easy to tell she was making Cooper uncomfortable, too."

I choke out a bitter laugh. "Yeah, well, not uncomfortable enough, considering he didn't push her away."

"You're right. He should have."

"He fucking lied to me, Julia. He said he hasn't had anything to do with her since they broke up."

"Maybe he was over at her house for another reason?"

I shake my head, dismissing the suggestion immediately. No way, it didn't sound like that at all. I glance over at her. "Do you still have the invitation to that party in Callingwood?"

She hesitates. "Yes. It's in my purse, but I sort of told Jax I wouldn't go since you told Cooper you weren't going."

"Yeah, well, that promise to him is out the fucking window now, but you don't have to come. I can drop you off at home on my way. I would completely understand, but I need to get out of here, Jules. I need to get my mind off of what just happened back there."

She shakes her head. "Of course I'm coming. I'll drive home if you want to have a few drinks."

"Thanks," I whisper, glad that she always has my back. Because that is exactly what I want to do—I want to party my ass off and forget this night ever happened, and more importantly, I want to forget about Cooper McKay. Though I doubt any amount of alcohol will ever erase him from me, especially my heart.

An hour later, I realize this was a mistake, because no matter how much I drink or how much I try to mingle, nothing lifts the heaviness that's weighing down on my chest.

People bump into me from either side as I make my way through the heavy crowd to find Julia. Some stop to hug me and ask how I'm doing, some try to get me to join their drinking game, and suddenly it all becomes too much.

I dart to the left and push my way through the crowded bodies until I finally make it into the deserted woods. The loud music starts to fade as I walk a little ways in, finding the privacy I need. I take a seat against one of the big oak trees and try to get my head together, but the quiet has me thinking about the night's earlier events. Hugging my knees to my chest, I let my tears flow freely, and try to think of how I'm going to make it up to my parents. As for Cooper… I shake my head, the pain is too much to think about it right now, but I know what I have to do.

The sound of a branch snapping has my head shooting up, and I see none other than Mark fucking Stevens stumbling toward me.

Great, just what I need.

"Well, hey there, Goldilocks." The nickname I was given back in grade school by my peers slurs out of his drunk mouth.

"Keep walking, Mark, I'm not in the mood for your shit tonight," I mumble and swipe at my wet cheeks, hating for anyone to see me cry.

He clutches at his chest dramatically. "Your words cut me deep."

I roll my eyes at his theatrics.

He makes his way over to me, completely ignoring my brush-off, and takes the spot next to me. "Here, have some of this. It will make you feel better," he says, thrusting his drink toward me.

"No, thanks."

He dances the cup closer to my face. "Come on, take it, I know you want it."

I push his wrist away with a chuckle. "Get the hell out of here. God, you're annoying. Anyone ever tell you that?"

"Only the ladies that want me." I shake my head at his arrogance. "What's going on, Kellar? Not like you to cry."

"Yeah, because you know me so well."

"I do," he replies insulted. "I've known you almost my entire life."

"You have gone to school with me most of your life, that doesn't mean you know me."

"I know you never cry, and I know that Julia is your best friend." I quirk a brow at him. "I'm not just a pretty face," he says, tapping his cheek. I turn my face away, trying to hide my smile from him. "I can actually be a good listener, if you give me a chance."

Silence consumes us as I think about it. Am I seriously considering talking to him about this? I look back at him to see him watching me, and he smirks when he knows he's got me.

I grab his drink from him and take a hefty sip of some nasty shit then hand it back. Blowing out a heavy breath, I drop my head back on the tree, look up at the starlit sky, and think about tonight's events. "Have you ever done something you aren't proud of, no matter how good it felt at the time?" I think about my question then laugh. "Never mind, what am I saying—of course you have."

He grunts, clearly not finding my remark as funny as me. "Nope, I don't waste my time regretting shit, Goldilocks, and you shouldn't either. Life is too short. Besides, whatever you did, I'm sure it's not that bad."

I keep silent, because I disagree. What I did probably ruined any chance of my father getting that contract, something he deserves to have, and it was all done out of pain and anger.

"Is this about that pig you have a thing for?"

I tense at his remark about Cooper. "Don't talk about him like that. Not ever, and especially not to me."

He grunts again. "I figured. You need to get over him, Goldilocks, that prick is so full of himself, you will never be good enough for him."

I try not to let his words cut me but they do, deeply. I glare back at him. "You're a real asshole, you know that?"

I begin to get up but he grabs my arm and pulls me back down. "Whoa, hold up now. I didn't mean it because you aren't good enough. I just meant that, to him, you never will be. That asshole thinks his shit don't stink, and it's because he's been labeled the town golden boy ever since he moved here, all because of who his daddy is."

I think about his statement and realize it's partly true. Cooper's dad grew up here and was the town's legend when it came to football. He even went on to play pro for a few years. When the star quarterback returned to coach the high school football team, Cooper was immediately lumped into the same category as his father. Especially after proving his talents on the field by bringing home state championships two years in a row. I guess Cooper is partly labeled the town golden boy because of his father but he also deserves that title. Even though I am pissed at him, there is no denying that he is a good guy. One day he will become Sunset Bay's sheriff and I have no doubt he will be a good one. Besides my father, he's the best man I know… Ugh! Now I feel like crying all over again.

I'm suddenly pulled out of my thoughts when I feel Mark's hand grasp the inside of my thigh. I immediately slap it away and glare at him. "What the hell are you doing?"

An irritating smirk tilts his lips. "I'm trying to get your mind off your troubles. Come on, Goldilocks, fuck him out of your system, I'm a willing participant."

I gape at him when I realize he's completely serious. Shaking my head, I expel a bitter laugh. "God, and here I thought just maybe you actually had a decent bone in your body, but I guess not." I try to get up again but he grabs my arm, a little rougher than before, and pulls me back down. "Get your fucking hand off me before I break it."

"Come on, don't be like that." He leans in to kiss me, and I smack him across the face, hard enough that it stings my hand.

"I told you to back off!"

I attempt to stand again but this time he grabs me by my hair. "I don't think so, bitch." He yanks me back down, drawing a startled cry from me. All of a sudden I'm on my stomach with his weight over top of me and panic immediately floods my system.

"Get off of me!" I kick and fight with everything I have to get free but I'm not strong enough, and I quickly realize I'm in real trouble here. I start to scream but he shoves my face into the ground, the rough earth biting painfully into my cheek.

"Just stay still, and I promise I will make it better."

My teeth clench in rage. I quickly spot a big rock only an arm's length away. As he fumbles with my pants, I'm able to slip my arm out from under me and grab it. Somehow, I manage to wiggle and turn myself over just enough so that I can swing the rock and connect it with his face. A painful howl leaves him, and I take quick advantage of his shock to slide myself out from underneath him. He grabs my ankle to drag me back but I'm able to kick free. As soon as I get on my feet, I haul ass.

"You fucking bitch!"

I glance back and see him getting up to chase after me. Panic has me pushing myself faster. I begin screaming, as I get closer to the party, hoping someone will hear me. I turn back to find out how close Mark is but I don't see him, then suddenly, I slam into a brick wall. Arms quickly grab me to steady me, and my fear has me fighting to get free, thinking somehow he ended up in front of me.

"Kayla! Stop, it's me!"

I look up through my blurry vision and realize it's Cooper. "Oh thank god," I sob in relief.

He grasps my chin and his eyes widen in alarm when he sees my face. "What the fuck happened to you?"

Before I can explain, Jaxson and Julia come running up. "Oh my god, Kayla, are you okay?" Julia asks.

I nod through my tears, my chest still heaving for breath. Cooper's gaze trains on something behind me, his eyes turning wild with rage.

I spin around to see Mark come to an abrupt stop, not looking much better than me. "You have got to be shitting me," he says in disbelief.

Cooper quickly puts the pieces together and starts toward him. "You're fucking dead!" He grabs Mark by the shirt and throws him up against the closest tree.

Jaxson moves fast and pulls him back before he can do any real damage. "Easy, man, find your control, there is a lot at stake here."

Cooper pushes away from him but Jaxson makes sure to stay close.

"What are you going to do?" Mark asks with a cocky smirk, spreading his arms out at his sides. "You gonna hit me, pig? Do it. I fucking dare you."

Even from here I can see Cooper's body vibrating with fury. I start over as he takes another step toward Mark and put my hand on his chest. "Don't, he's only trying to bait you. Let's just get out of here. Please."

Mark chuckles. "Listen to the bitch and leave, because we both know you can't do shit."

In one heart-stopping second, I see Cooper wind back, and I know he's going to hit him. Panic has my protest lodging in my throat, but thankfully, Jaxson is quicker than Cooper. "He can't, but I can." A split second later you hear fist connecting with flesh and Mark falls to the ground from Jaxson's blow, blood pouring from his nose.

"Fuck! You broke my nose, you asshole! I'm pressing charges."

Cooper drops down to look him in the face. "You're not going to do anything because there are no witnesses to back up your story, but I wonder what your daddy will say when he has to try and dismiss an attempted rape charge from your record." He grabs Mark's jaw now, and by the whimper that escapes him, I can tell it's hard. "Listen up, you little fuck. If you ever come near her again, I will make sure you regret it for the rest of your life. There is only so far I will be pushed, and believe me when I say this is not over." Cooper shoves his head down in the ground as he stands then looks over at me, his eyes flat and void of any emotion. "Let's go."

"Cooper…" I start with a whisper, but he doesn't give me a chance to speak.

"No! We aren't talking about this right now. Go!"

I swallow past the urge to argue, but know now is not the time. Julia links arms with me as we start to walk off with Cooper and Jaxson following close behind. I hear them talking in hushed tones, and although I can't hear what they're saying, there is no denying the quiet fury in Cooper's voice.

As soon as we make it to the party, I ignore everyone and beeline for my car, making Julia jog to have to keep up.

"Jules! You come with me." I glance over at Jaxson to see him wave her over to Cooper's truck that is parked in front of mine.

"Do you want me to stay with you? I will and tell Jax no. He's pissed at me anyway."

I look over at Cooper to see him on his phone, and vaguely hear him reporting the party. He shakes his head at me, as if he knows what I'm thinking, then makes his way over to us. "Yeah, and find Stevens as soon as you get here and search him. I'll meet up with you in a bit."

I tune him out then look back at Julia. "No, it's okay, go ahead. I'm sorry I got you into shit for the second time this week," I whisper, feeling guilty.

She pulls me into a hug. "You didn't. We did nothing wrong coming here, Kayla. Call me when you get home and we will talk about what happened with Mark, okay?"

I nod and hug her tighter, not wanting to let her go because I'm not ready to deal with Cooper quite yet. She kisses my cheek before stepping back, but hesitates to walk away when she sees my face. "Kayla, are you sure? I'll drive you home and we can talk. The guys will get over it."

I attempt to give her a reassuring smile. "I'm sure. Really, it's fine. I need to talk to him anyway."

"Okay, make sure you call me as soon as you get home."

"I will."

She starts off toward Jaxson and I get in the passenger side of my car since Cooper is in the driver's seat. I hand him my keys and he takes them in silence, then pulls away and stares straight ahead. The confined space is thick with tension but it's a different tension than what it was a few days ago, after Brittany's car incident. I glance at him and my stomach twists at his stoic expression. I've seen him mad before, but nothing like this. I swipe at my subsiding tears, flinching as I pass over my sore cheek.

When we are over halfway home, and he still hasn't said anything, I decide to break the silence. "So what, Cooper, you came all this way and you're not even going to say anything to me?"

"It's best if we don't talk right now." His response has my irritation reaching a whole new level.

"For who? You?"

"No! For you!" I flinch at his angry bellow. There is a moment of silence before he slams his fist down on the steering wheel. "Fuck!" He runs his hand through his hair in frustration, his breathing fast and heavy. "You fucking promised me you wouldn't go!"

I grind my teeth and try to keep my temper in check. "Yeah, well you promised me things too, and you lied."

"I never lied to you!"

"Yes, you did! You said you had nothing to do with her since you broke up. Oh, but I guess going to her house for supper and her lake house with her doesn't count, huh?"

His jaw flexes. "She's full of shit! I was at her house for supper because of the fucking vandalism on her car and her parents asked me to stay. Any time before that was business, since her dad is on the town council. And I wasn't there alone, I was there with Sheriff Lancaster. It was her parents who invited me to their lake house at supper last night and I declined. This is all shit you would have known if you stuck around to hear me out."

"What do you expect, Cooper? Not even two nights ago you had your fingers inside of me, and then I was subjected to watching her put her hands all over you, without you even attempting to stop it."

"You think that shit wasn't uncomfortable for me, too?"

"Oh yeah, you looked really uncomfortable."

"What the fuck was I supposed to do? I didn't want to ruin supper for your parents. If I had known they were going to be there then I wouldn't have come!"

"You should have pushed her away regardless. Try being in my position. Do you really think I was going to stay a second longer to witness any more of that shit?"

"If you would have stuck around then you would have heard me lay into her, right in front of everyone for what she did. And you would have also seen your dad go to bat for you, too. But no, you had to be fucking impulsive again, like always, and let your emotions get the better of you."

My anger deflates fast, and I sit in stunned silence as we pull onto my driveway. I'm shocked to know that not only did Cooper stand up for me in front of everyone, but so did my dad. Guilt plagues me, and I'm just about to thank him but he doesn't give me the chance.

"Do you have any idea the positions you put me in because you can't ever think shit through? I lied about not knowing who did that shit to her car, which is the first time I have ever done that, and I fucking hate it. Now, I almost just beat the shit out of a kid because you took off on a tantrum and got yourself into trouble that I warned you from to begin with. I mean jesus, it's like fucking poison wherever you go!"

The last of his words strike me like a painful blow. It's so intense I swear my heart just stopped beating and I have a hard time pulling in a breath. Mark's remark earlier about not being good enough for him rings loudly in my ears, and I'm not sure what hurts more—that he was right or that Cooper really does think this.

I do everything in my power to hold my tears back and swallow past the excruciating burn in my throat. "You're right," I whisper, staring straight ahead. "I am impulsive, especially when I'm hurt. I have a temper that spikes from zero to ten in one second and sometimes that makes it really hard to think things through. But what you're most right about is I am not good for you. Or maybe I should say not good *enough* for you." I laugh bitterly. "Who the fuck knew that Mark would be right about something tonight after all."

I open the car door and hear him expel a heavy breath. "Kayla."

"I will fix the mess I made, and I promise to stay the hell away from you and not subject you to my *poison* ever again."

I slam the door and rush into my house, refraining from looking back, the heartache that's crawling up my throat threatening to choke me. I enter the kitchen on the way to my room and see my parents waiting for me at the table.

I stop to face them but have a hard time looking at them, especially my dad. My mom gasps when she sees my face, but I'm not sure if it's because of my bruised cheek or if the pain I'm feeling is apparent.

"Honey, what happened to you? Where did you go?" she asks.

I open my mouth to try and explain but then snap it shut as I feel my heartbreak erupting to the surface. I swallow and try again, but look at my dad this time. "I'm sorry, dad. I'm so sorry." He moves to stand, but I shake my head at him. "No, please. I—I can't talk right now. I will explain everything later, I promise, but I just can't right now."

I rush up to my room as a strangled noise leaves my throat, but manage to hold the dam off until I fall into bed. I hug my pillow close and try to muffle my sobs. I let everything pour out of me. My humiliation and guilt for what happened at supper, my anger at Mark, but mostly I cry my heart out over Cooper. For the fact that I wasted three years loving someone who never thought I was good enough anyway.

I mean jesus, it's like fucking poison wherever you go!

I meant what I said—I will fix the mess I made, then I will make sure to never taint him again.

CHAPTER 5

A couple nights later, I'm sitting out on the back patio in my sweats with a blanket draped around me, the warm night and clear starlit sky doing nothing for my heavy heart. I hear the back door open, then a second later my mom takes the chair next to me and hands me a cup of tea. I smile at her as I take the steaming mug then curl my feet under me and look ahead into the distance again. I feel her watch me and know we are about to have the talk that I've been stalling.

"Mr. Vail called your father." I falter, not expecting her to start with that. "He said you went there today and apologized, not only about what happened at supper but also about Brittany's car."

My blood heats when I think about apologizing to that bitch. Her parents were good about it, but she was smug as shit and enjoyed every minute of my humiliation. I hate that my parents found out from Mr. Vail and not me. I didn't think he would call them, especially not so soon.

"Yeah, it wasn't easy but I knew it was the right thing to do," I admit.

"Yes, it was the right thing to do, but I wouldn't have held it against you if you didn't."

I tear my gaze away from the darkness and look at my mom now, surprised by her comment. "You wouldn't?"

"No, because you're right, Brittany is a class A bitch."

I rear back, shocked by her language. A moment of stunned silence stretches between us before we both burst out laughing. It's the first time I've laughed or smiled in days and it feels really good, but I sober quickly. "Yeah, she is, but I shouldn't have let her bait me like that. I hate that I ruined things for Dad."

She shakes her head with a smile. "You didn't ruin anything, honey. Your dad got that contract."

"He did?"

"He did. That is partly why Mr. Vail called him. He also told your father that he had a very courageous daughter and that he should be really proud of her. Of course, we both already knew that."

I smile and feel some of the guilt lift from me, knowing that I didn't screw things up beyond repair. "Well, I'm glad one good thing came out of this."

My mom's expression softens and I already know what she's about to say before she says it. "How on earth did I not know about your feelings for Cooper?"

Just the sound of his name is like a blow to the stomach. "It's not like I was really forthcoming about it."

"No, but when I think about it now, it's clear as day. I hate how oblivious I was and that I didn't know my baby was in love."

I swallow thickly and feel tears sting my eyes but I hold them back, I've shed enough over the last few days.

"I really hate that I invited him here with the Vails. I hope you know I would have never done that had I known."

"Of course I do. Don't worry about it, Mom, none of it matters anymore anyway," I tell her softly.

"Oh, and why do you say that?"

It takes me a minute to find my words. "Because I'm not good enough for him, and in his eyes I never will be." I turn my face away and bite my lip, trying to stop it from quivering.

"Kayla Kellar, look at me right now!" I turn back to her with a blurry gaze and swipe at the single tear that manages to slip free. My mom's expression is sad as she cups my face. "You listen to me, you are wrong. You're more than good enough for Cooper."

"We are so different, too different. Cooper is so levelheaded and I'm…not."

"Of course you're different. It wouldn't be fun otherwise." I shake my head but she doesn't let me speak. "Yes, you have a hot temper, and sometimes that makes you react without thinking, but you come by it honestly, and you have your father to thank for it." I can't help but smile at that because I know it's the truth. "Never doubt your self-worth, Kayla. I think you and Cooper are perfect for each other, and I'm happy to know out of all the people you could have fallen for it was him."

My smile vanishes and pain lances through me again. "It doesn't matter. Not anymore. He doesn't feel the same way."

"You're wrong. I saw it that night. He was so panicked when you ran out like that. He really laid into Brittany and so did your father. He wouldn't have done that if he didn't care." I don't say anything because I know she doesn't understand and she isn't going to. "I don't know what happened with you guys the other night, but I hate seeing you so heartbroken. Whatever it is, I know y'all can fix it."

I shake my head again, my throat too tight to speak. Some things can't be undone.

She expels a heavy breath then leans in and kisses my cheek. "Just think about it, sweetheart. Finish your tea then come inside and see your father. He's worried about you."

I nod. "Okay, I will."

She gives me one more kiss then goes inside. I stare into the darkness again and think about everything she had to say. She doesn't understand because she doesn't know what he said. And when I really think about it, I'm starting to realize this is all for the best, no matter how much it hurts. I am irrational and let my emotions get the best of me. It's just how I'm wired, and the future sheriff of Sunset Bay doesn't need that kind of hassle. He is going to have responsibilities and an image to uphold, he doesn't need my *poison*.

I shake myself out of my thoughts and worry about a different set of problems, like the fact that prom is this coming weekend and I'm all alone with no date, and I have no one to blame but myself. I was so happy for Julia that she finally got the courage to ask Jaxson, and even more elated that he said yes. She told me to come with them, but no way in hell am I being their third wheel. There isn't enough time for me to find anyone else to go with, everyone already has dates. Well, maybe not Timmy Dickerhoff, but there is no way I'm going to subject myself to his creepiness just so I'm not dateless. I'd rather not go at all.

The sound of a familiar truck pulls in next door, and I immediately get the urge to run into the house but I don't want to give him the satisfaction. I'm glad his parents get home tomorrow and I won't have to see him so often anymore. I tense in surprise at the sound of my gate opening and my heart races anxiously.

Why the hell is he coming over here?

I feel his gaze on me as he makes his way over, and I curse my body's reaction to it.

"Hey," he greets quietly.

"Hi."

I hear him take the seat next to me, but I keep my eyes forward and don't look over at him. "How have you been?"

"Fine."

In my peripheral vision I see him shift uncomfortably. "We didn't get a chance to talk about what happened with Mark the other night."

I tense, not wanting to have this conversation with him. "I don't want to talk about it, Cooper. Especially with you."

He releases a frustrated breath. "Then will you at least go to the station tomorrow and talk to someone else? Leave a statement? He was arrested that night for having drugs on him, but he needs to pay for what he did to you, Kayla. For whatever the fuck happened. And since I can't punish him with my fists, I will make him pay with the law."

I take a moment to think about this. I haven't told my parents yet about what happened with Mark, but Cooper is right, I do need to make a statement. The last thing I want to happen is for Mark to do this to some other girl because I never spoke up. Hell, who's to say he hasn't already done this to someone else. They just may not have been as lucky as I was.

"I'll go tomorrow."

I hear him expel another breath, this one sounding more like relief. "Good. Thanks." When I stay silent, he clears his throat. "So, I heard you went and saw the Vails today."

Of course he did.

"Yep, but don't worry, I didn't say you caught us. I left yours and Julia's name out of it."

I feel the intensity of his eyes as he watches me, and I desperately want to look over at him but I don't, knowing it will only make it harder. Even his delicious scent is getting to me right now, making it difficult to hold on to my resolve, and that just jacks my annoyance up another notch.

"I didn't think you would have."

"No?" I question, trying to keep the sarcasm out of my tone. "Then why are you bringing it up? Shocked that I have a decent bone in my body, Cooper?"

"Jesus, no, that's not it. I—"

"Save it. I don't care, it doesn't matter anymore."

"The hell it doesn't! Would you fucking look at me?"

I shake my head and stand, not wanting to be around him right now. I'm still too upset to talk to him. He grabs my wrist with a frustrated growl and electricity shoots through my arm like a bolt of lightning. I look at where he has me grasped, then for the first time I look up at him, and like I thought, just the sight of him hurts. “Better be careful, Cooper, there’s only so much *poison* someone can take before it kills them.” I know it’s a bitter thing to say but I can’t help it, I’m still so hurt by his words. Words I will never forget.

I ignore the guilt that washes over his expression. “I didn’t mean it, Kayla.”

“Yes, you did. Because, unlike me, you aren’t irrational, and you only ever say what you mean.”

I rip out of his grasp and rush into my house, ignoring him when he calls me back. It hurts like hell but I know in the end it’s better this way. I can’t let myself love him anymore; he already made it clear that I’m not good enough. Prolonging this will only end up breaking me in the end.

CHAPTER 6

My heart races and my stomach twists anxiously as I pull up in front of the banquet hall. My phone buzzes like crazy but I don't look at it, knowing it's probably Julia. I feel so guilty for telling her last minute that I would just meet her here and not go to her house first, but I just couldn't show up with her and Jaxson. I would have felt like a complete idiot. Though, maybe it wouldn't have mattered, because as I get out of my car and see all the couples laughing and walking up to the front doors, I still feel like an idiot.

I feel a panic attack coming on and second-guess the decision I made to come here. So instead of heading into the hall, I dart to the right and follow the stone path that leads to a beautiful garden lit up with white lights. I come to a sudden stop when I see a couple kissing, thinking they're in privacy. I'm about to turn back around but they end up breaking apart and start leaving first.

"Hey, Kayla," Suzy greets me with a blissful smile. "You look amazing, I love your dress."

I glance down at my dress, the one my mom and I shopped hours for. At the time I had hoped to find something that would knock Cooper on his ass. The soft, black silk hugs my body in all the right places and falls effortlessly in others. The trim of rhinestones lay delicately along the swells of my breasts then follows a path along the straps and outlines the seams of the open back. Yep, it's pretty fucking epic, and I have no one to impress with it.

Ugh, get over it, Kayla.

I paste a fake smile on my face. “Thanks, I love yours, too. You guys both look great.”

“Thanks.” They head to the back entrance, and I hear the music faintly as he opens the door for her and they enter the hall.

Blowing out a heavy breath, I go take a seat on the cement bench that’s in front of a small fountain. The sound of the water and the warmth of the surrounding white lights begin to calm my erratic heartbeat.

God, what was I thinking coming here? Would it really have mattered to miss my own prom?

My entire week has already been shit; missing this wouldn’t have made it much worse. Between having to tell my parents about what happened with Mark, going to the police station to file a report, and ensuring Cooper wouldn’t be there at the same time has left me completely drained. I should have just stayed home, curled up in bed, and watched *Dirty Dancing* while vegging out and cursing a certain sexy cop. The idea sounds more appealing by the second and I decide that’s exactly what I’m going to do. I’m in no mood to be here and my pity party is only going to wreck it for others.

Standing, I turn and start walking but come to an abrupt halt when I see someone come charging in frantically. “There you are!”

My eyes widen in shock, and I blink several times, thinking I’m hallucinating the person in front of me.

“Why aren’t you answering your damn phone?” Cooper asks through labored breaths. He’s bent down with his hands on his knees, looking like he just ran a marathon. He holds a corsage in his hand that looks a little worse for wear.

Silence surrounds us as I gape at him, still not believing what I’m seeing.

After catching his breath, he stands to his full height and his eyes sweep down my body. “Jesus, you look fucking incredible.”

My stomach does a flip at his compliment and blatant appreciation, but I wish it didn't. *Bastard.* He's a sexy bastard, especially all dressed up, but still…

"What are you doing here?" I ask, finally finding my words.

He starts toward me, or maybe stalks is a better word. His eyes are narrowed and he looks insanely pissed. "You were supposed to go to Julia's first. You ruined my plan."

I rear back, aghast at his reply. "Well, I changed my mind. You and your plans weren't a part of it. Just like they aren't now, which is why I'm leaving."

I move to walk around him but before I can make it past him, he wraps an arm around my waist and pulls me back against him. Heat rushes through my veins, and I suck in a sharp breath when I feel his erection against my lower back.

"Cooper, let me go." The protest is weak at best. My heart has me never wanting to leave this spot in his arms, but my pride and hurt feelings tell me to run as fast and far as I can.

"No! I'm not letting you run away again."

"Please don't do this," I plead on a shaky whisper. "I can't take any more this week."

I feel his body soften behind me. "Please just hear me out, baby."

Oh the bastard just had to use 'baby', didn't he?

He takes my silence as a yes, which I guess it is, then takes a seat on the bench where I was just sitting and pulls me down on his lap, his obvious erection now nestled along my ass. The stubborn side of me wants to wiggle my way out of his arms but the other side, the wounded one that has missed him so much, wants to burrow closer. Instead, I sit stock-still, stare at the flowing water and try to steel myself against the conflicting emotions battling inside of me. But I don't have much luck when his arms hug me closer and I feel his lips on my bare back.

"I'm sorry, Kayla. I'm so sorry for what I said, I didn't mean it." I open my mouth to argue but he quickly claps a hand over it. "Please, just let me finish, if you still want to yell at me after I'm done then fine. But just hear me out first."

My protest deflates and I slump in his arms.

He removes his hand and continues. "I was really pissed off that night, and I wasn't even all that upset at you. I was mad at Brittany for being a bitch and hurting you. I was pissed off and worried when I found out from Jaxson that you were at that party. Then when I found you there, running scared, with your face messed up like that…" He trails off and drops his forehead on my back with a heavy breath. "I was furious, Kayla, and I snapped. I fucking hated that I couldn't beat the shit out of that prick, and hated even more that I almost lost control, which would have ended my career. The entire night was a giant clusterfuck, and I said things that I didn't mean."

I take a moment to absorb everything he just said. I get it. If anyone understands saying things in the heat of the moment it's me, but it doesn't lessen the sting of what he said. "I understand how you were feeling, because I felt the exact same way most of the night, but what you said, Cooper, was harsh and it really hurt me."

"I know. I swear if I could take it back—"

I turn and cut him off by putting my hand over his mouth. "It's my turn now."

I feel him grin. "Sorry, baby, continue."

I begin to remove my hand but before I can, he encloses his fingers around my wrist and kisses my palm, the entire gesture warming my heart. His light green eyes are soft and pleading, but I try to steel myself against it because this needs to be said.

"I'm not sure it matters anymore, because I'm never going to change. This is who I am. I'm irrational, and I get pissed off quickly. I jump to conclusions, and I really don't have much self-control, but that's not all of who I am. I'm a good person, Cooper, despite what you think, and I usually only get irrational like that when it comes to people I care about."

His eyes fall closed and he drops his forehead on my shoulder again, but not before I see pain flash through them. "You're the best person I know, Kayla, and I fucking hate that I made you think otherwise. If I could take it back I would, but I swear I'll make it up to you. I promise to make sure you never doubt my feelings again."

"And what are your feelings?" His head snaps up, and I force myself to hold his gaze, then taking a deep breath, I gather my courage and voice my feelings. "As much as I want you, I need to understand where you're coming from. This isn't some crush for me, I've loved you for a long time," I admit softly. "And if you don't intend for this to be more than you working me out of your system then I can't do it. I'm sorry but I can't."

His eyes bore into mine and my heart jackhammers in my chest as I wait to see if I will be rejected. I expected to see some alarm in his gaze from my admission of the 'L' word, but shockingly, I don't.

He reaches up and cups the side of my face, his thumb tracing delicately along my bottom lip. "You are the biggest pain in the ass." I frown at his unexpected response. "But you are my pain in the ass," he quickly adds with a smirk. "You always have been, and I don't want you to change for anything." His smile vanishes as he lets out a heavy breath. "There are reasons why we couldn't be together until now, ones that really matter to me. Yeah, I could have dated you, but I know that I wouldn't have had the self-control to keep my dick in my pants. But make no mistake of my feelings for you, Kayla. You've weaved your stubborn ass so deep inside of me there will be no working you out of my system, baby, and tonight everything changes for us."

Joy explodes through my chest, and I drop my forehead on his with relief. I stare into his intense gaze, my lips only a breath from his. "I'm good at weaving my stubborn ass inside of people, it's a gift."

He smirks then turns his face into the side of my neck and trails his lips up my throat. "Do you forgive me, baby?"

"Mmm, maybe," I whisper as I tilt my head to the side for him.

"Come on, even perfect assholes like me make mistakes sometimes."

"Pffft," I harrumph.

With a chuckle, he leans back then frames my face before drawing my mouth down to his. I gasp at the first touch of his lips, it's completely electrifying and soul touching. I weave my fingers through his hair to hold him close and let his kiss ease the wounds that were engraved on my heart this past week.

His tongue wastes no time thrusting past my lips, demanding more, and I happily give him the access he wants. I whimper as his delicious flavor floods my senses, one that I have craved and dreamed about since that night on his parents' kitchen table. "Goddamn, I love the way you taste." His big, warm hand slides up my high slit and grasps my upper thigh. "And this dress is going to drive me fucking crazy all damn night."

"It doesn't have to," I mumble breathlessly. "Let's go back to your place and you can rip it off me, or hell, just hike that shit up and do all the dirty things you want to me."

He chuckles but it trails off into a groan. "No, I'm not letting you miss your prom, but I promise, baby, you're going to feel me tonight. Everywhere. My mouth, my hands, my cock—all of it. I'm going to claim what's mine, what has always been mine."

My panties flood with arousal at his possessive words, and I desperately want to hike my dress up, crawl on top of him, and have him claim every part of me right here, right now. I consider doing just that but he ends up pulling away and stands us up.

"No, don't stop." I jump and cling to him like a dog in heat then crush my mouth to his again.

His hands cup my silk-covered ass as he lifts me off my feet with a growl. "We have to stop or I'm going to come in my fucking pants."

"That's okay, it will feel good, take the edge off until we go back to your place."

He expels a tortured groan. "Jesus, Kayla, I'm trying to do the right thing here, help a guy out."

"Sometimes it pays to be bad, Coop." I press on, hoping to convince him.

"Oh believe me, there is nothing good about anything I plan to do to you tonight, but"—he drops me back down to my feet—"not until midnight."

I huff in frustration and blow a stray curl out of my face. "Fine, then let's get this show on the road so we can get out of here." I grab his hand to drag him behind me but he doesn't budge and ends up yanking me back against him.

"Hold up," he whispers in my ear, sending shivers along my spine. "I have something for you." He picks up the mangled looking corsage off the bench and slides it on my wrist. "Sorry it's a fucking mess, it got wrecked when I was running from my truck that I had to park a mile away."

I smile down at it. "It's perfect."

"You're lying, it's shit."

"You're right, it is," I admit with a giggle. "But it is perfect to me because it's from you."

I feel his smile against my cheek before his lips brush it softly. "Come on, baby, let's go inside. Jaxson and Julia are saving seats for us." Linking our fingers together, I start leading the way, when suddenly I hear him groan behind me. I glance back to see him staring at the open back of my dress. "This is going to be the longest fucking night of my life."

He's got that right.

We make our way into the banquet hall and are immediately assaulted with loud music and a sea of bodies. We wind our way through the crowd to find Jaxson and Julia at one of the tables in the center of the room. Julia stands then meets me halfway and pulls me in for a hug. "Everything okay?" she asks in my ear.

I squeeze her back tightly. "Yeah, actually, everything is perfect."

She steps back and gives me a big smile. "Looks like we got our wish," she says, glancing over at the guys. "Well, you got yours, I only got half of mine, but at least he's here with me."

"It will happen one day, Jules, I know it." And I do, because I see the way he looks at her, everyone does. "Come on." I sling my arm around her shoulders as we walk over to the table.

The first half of the night surprisingly speeds along and I'm having a good time. We take pictures, Julia and I dance while the guys glare at anyone who comes near us. At one point I thought Bobby Wright was a dead man when he started dancing behind Julia, but with one look from Jaxson he backed his ass right to the other side of the dance floor. As the night wears on, I become more anxious for midnight to hit. Every time Cooper looks at me, his eyes are intense and hold promise. Every gentle touch, whether it is on my leg or back, has tremors racing along my skin and my body humming with arousal.

After the announcement of prom queen and king, we decided to pick up a pizza and go to the beach where Jaxson and Julia always hang out. Cooper and I went in my car while Jaxson drove his truck, and it took some major self-control on my part not to maul the sexy bastard on the way over. But I knew it would only make it harder on the both of us. I understand now how important it is for him to wait until that clock strikes midnight.

So here we are, the four of us sitting in front of the ocean, our feet in the warm sand and the ocean breeze misting across our faces while we chow down on pizza from Antonio's. Both Julia and I are wearing the guys' jackets since it's a little cooler this close to the water.

Once we finish eating, Cooper pulls me between his legs. I lean back against his hard chest and try not to moan when I feel his erection against my lower back.

Jesus, has that bad boy been like this all night?

When Julia walks back from throwing out our garbage, she goes to take the seat next to Jaxson but he surprises us both by pulling her in the same way Cooper has me. I watch her soft expression break out into the biggest smile.

"So, girls, how does it feel to almost be done with school for the rest of your lives?" Cooper asks.

"It feels a little weird," I reply first. "If you think about it we have been in the same routine for the last twelve years, thirteen if you want to count kindergarten. Wake up early and go to school, every Monday you pray for it to be Friday, you look forward to the weekends and summers but also love seeing your friends at school every day. As much as I'm going to enjoy not having schoolwork anymore, I don't think I'm really feeling this bill business that will start coming my way soon. I'm quite content to have my dad still buy me everything."

They all chuckle but what they don't realize is I'm partly serious.

Who the hell wants to grow up and have more responsibilities?

Well, okay, Cooper makes it a little more appealing. I'm assuming he wouldn't be cool with me living off my dad forever.

"Well, I'm not done with school yet," Julia says, cutting into my thoughts. "If I get into the University of Charleston I will have four more years of it. But I have decided to take a year off because, like you said, I need a break after twelve years.

"You didn't tell me that," Jaxson says in surprise.

"I just decided a few days ago after talking with Grams about it." She pauses then turns back to look up at him. "Why? You don't think it's a good idea?"

"I think it's a great idea. Take a break, have fun for a year then go to college. I have no doubt that you will get in and end up being the best teacher any kid can have."

She smiles up at him. "Thanks, Jax."

He leans down and gives her a kiss on the forehead.

I roll my eyes and shake my head. Seriously, how can she not see this shit?

"Have you given any more thought to those business courses? It sounds like Eddie really wants you to take over the shop for him," she says, talking about the mechanic shop he works at.

There's a slight pause, and out of the corner of my eye I see him briefly glance over at Cooper before he clears his throat. "No, not yet."

What is that all about?

"That's okay, you have time," she replies with a shrug, missing the exchange.

A comfortable silence settles over us as we listen to the sound of the waves crash against the shore, but I swear I can hear a clock ticking every second. I know Cooper does too, since he's checking his watch constantly. The last time he checks it, I lean over and see we still have a half hour. I hear him blow out a frustrated breath behind me. "You know what, fuck it." Before I can register his words, he hauls me up to my feet. "We're out of here, we'll catch up with you guys tomorrow."

He yanks on my hand to propel me forward but I plant my feet in the sand then reach down and swipe my shoes. I barely have them snagged when he pulls on me again. "Bye," I yell back to Jaxson and Julia with a wave.

"Yeah, I won't be going home tonight," Jaxson grumbles behind me.

I hear Julia giggle but can't make out what she says since Cooper is pulling me at a fast pace.

"Coop, slow down, this dress wasn't made for running."

Instead of listening, he turns back and catches me off guard by picking me up around the waist. With a squeal of surprise, I wrap my arms around his neck and laugh as he races to the car. I expect him to throw me in but instead he pins me against it then his mouth descends on mine. Moaning, I kiss him with the same desperation.

"I can't wait any longer," he mumbles against my lips. "I'll take you home and start fucking you with my mouth and hands until midnight, then you better be ready, baby, because it will be my cock next, and I have years of need to work out." He drives his statement home with a hard thrust against me, his erection hitting the little spot that has electricity shooting through every nerve ending in my body.

I'm about to beg him for it right here, right now, but I don't get the chance because he quickly deposits me in the car. When he peels away, I look over and see that he's going seven over the legal limit, the exact same speed he gave me a ticket for.

"Better be careful, Coop, or I will have to call you in. I know this cop who is a real stickler with that shit around these parts."

He grunts, not finding my sarcasm funny.

I think about the ticket that is sitting in my car. "I still can't believe you actually gave me a ticket."

There's a slight twitch to his lips. "If you would have gone to pay for the ticket already you would know it doesn't exist."

"Come again?" I ask, thinking I misunderstood him. "What do you mean it doesn't exist?"

"I mean exactly that. It's a fake."

My mouth drops open in shock. "Then why the hell did you even bother to give me one?"

"Because you needed to be put in your place for fucking with me like you did. And since I couldn't fuck the sass out of you, I decided to join in and play your little game." He looks over at me, his smirk spreading. "Except my way."

I gape at him, aghast. "What if I had gone to pay for it?"

He shrugs. "I made sure Cliff knew about it. I also told him that when you came in to make sure he called me. I didn't want to miss your reaction."

My eyes narrow at his smugness. *Why, the sneaky, clever bastard.*

Leaning over, my hand finds his erection through his dress pants. His grin vanishes, and I hear him inhale sharply.

"Mmm, too bad I didn't find out about this sooner, because I would have paid you back so good," I whisper in his ear. "If you thought the bikini in my hot tub was torture that's nothing to what you would have come home to find." I lick his earlobe. "Me, in your bed." *Nip.* "Waiting for you all naked and needy." *Nip.* "And since you wouldn't have touched me, I would have done it myself. I would have shown you exactly what I've done to myself for the last three years every time I thought about you."

Nothing less than a sound that you could describe as animalistic erupts deep from within his chest before he rips my hand away from him. "Oh, Kayla, you just played with some serious fire, baby, and you are going to get burned for it."

His threat has a fierce ache igniting between my thighs. Thankfully, we pull up to his place only a short minute later. Just as we enter his building, he picks me up then our hands and mouths are out of control once again. We bang against the hallway walls as we make our way to his door, refusing to have our lips apart from one another.

I release a startled yelp when he stumbles.

"Shit, fuck," he curses, but gains his footing quickly. "Sorry, baby, pretend that didn't happen."

I laugh into our kiss, loving that I make him feel this way—out of control, frantic, desperate—the same way he has always made me feel.

He pins me against the door as he fumbles to unlock it, then once we're in he slams it behind him. I feel us rush through his apartment just before the cool, soft mattress of his bed meets my back. I try to keep him close, but he doesn't allow it. He releases my mouth and quickly slips out of my arms, drawing a disappointed moan from me. I recover from it quickly though when his lips find the swells of my breasts. My nipples strain painfully under the silk of my dress, craving his attention. I push his head down when he takes too long, and feel him smile against my supple flesh just before his teeth graze my stiff peak through the thin material.

With a fiery moan I arch up for more, but he doesn't give it to me. Instead, the fucker tortures me, only giving me a tease over my dress, then lowers himself down my silk-covered body, bringing his mouth to the spot that I ache for him most. I feel his hands go to the slit just before he tears it higher, revealing my black panties. He brings his mouth against the wet lace and gives me a gentle kiss.

"Please, Cooper, I want more. I need more," I plead with a whimper.

"Soon, baby, but first you're going to back up that mouth of yours." I barely comprehend his words before he shreds my panties from my hips with one swift pull.

I gasp at the unexpected act but it quickly trails off on a moan.

Oh shit, that was so damn hot.

"Jesus, you're fucking perfect." My eyes fall closed when I feel his warm breath hit my bare center, and my hips rise—seeking his pleasure. When he doesn't give me the attention I want, I open my eyes to see him on his knees, staring up at me, right over my most intimate part. "Touch yourself, Kayla, show me how you have pleasured this sweet pussy while waiting for me."

Heat explodes through me at his erotic words. "I'll do it if you show me, too." I challenge.

He smiles at me, and it's a smile that has my heart skipping a beat. "You wanna see me stroke my cock, baby?"

I nod, my throat suddenly too dry to speak. He stands with confidence and rids himself of his shirt first, giving me a view that has my heart stalling in my chest.

God, he is beautiful.

His shoulders are broad and strong, his chest defined and his abs perfectly cut until they taper off into that sexy v—

"Get moving, Kayla."

My eyes snap to his, and I quirk a brow at the order. "My you're awfully bossy."

"I told you, baby, that's the only way it works with me in here."

"Hmmm, that you did. But just an FYI, the only time this is acceptable is when our clothes are off. Otherwise, don't press your luck."

"Like you are right now with that mouth of yours?"

I give him a wink, letting him know that's exactly what I'm doing.

"Stop stalling, Kayla."

I can tell I'm pushing it, so with a smile, I give him what he wants. I slowly trail my hand down between the center of my breasts and over the silk material. His heated gaze follows my path, warming me from the inside out. My hand freezes, hovering just above my destination, when Cooper moves to undo his belt, and I wait with bated breath for what I'm sure is going to be the sexiest thing I will ever see in my life. He unbuttons his dress slacks then drops his pants only enough to free himself.

All the air leaves my lungs at the first sight of his cock.

Oh sweet baby jesus and all that is holy, it's even bigger and hotter than I thought it would be.

"Now, Kayla, give me what I want." His gruff demand penetrates through my sexual fog. Continuing my descent, I reach down and slide two of my fingers through my wet flesh. A strangled noise escapes me as I find the bundle of nerves that's screaming for attention. "No. Don't stay there, keep moving, baby. Go inside. I wanna see your fingers fuck your tight little pussy."

I whimper, both at his dirty words and in need for wanting to give myself release, but I do as he says and enter both of my fingers deep inside of me. I gasp in pleasure at the snug feel and arch up into my hand.

A low growl penetrates through the heated silence. "That a girl, show me what you did while thinking about me." I pump my fingers in and out, all the while watching with rapt fascination as he strokes himself. "Do you like watching me stroke my cock, Kayla?"

"Yes," I answer truthfully, my voice barely above a whisper.

"This is what I have done almost every night while thinking about all the ways I was going to fuck you."

His words have fire erupting inside of me, my need for release so strong that it's painful. I bring the heel of my hand to grind against my throbbing clit. My stomach tightens and my breathing accelerates with my impending orgasm.

"No, stop." Cooper rips my hand away just before I detonate and it's enough to make me cry.

"Cooper, please. I—"

"Shhh. I got you." He drops to his knees in front of me then takes my two fingers into his mouth, sucking my arousal off of them and groans. "You taste as fucking good as I knew you would." Leaning down, he runs his warm, wet tongue through my aching center.

My entire body jolts off the bed and my fingers wind in his hair tightly, forcing him to stay exactly where he is.

He splays his hand along my lower tummy and holds me in place while he devours me like a starved man. I was already so close to exploding that I know I'm going to erupt at any moment. My feet find their place on his broad shoulders, and I thrust up against the perfection of his mouth.

"That's it, baby, fuck my mouth." His words vibrate against my clit and reverberate through my entire body.

"Oh god, I'm going to come. Right now." As soon as the words escape past my lips, he thrusts a single finger inside of me and it sends me crashing over the edge with an intensity that steals my breath. Ecstasy rushes through every nerve ending in my body and Cooper draws out my orgasm, making it last so long I think I could die from it. Once my final tremors subside, he eases his mouth away and kisses the inside of my thigh. I take a moment to try and steady my breathing as I float back down from the most intense orgasm I've ever had.

He stands, his pants still undone but his cock now back in his underwear. My eyes travel up his hard, bare body that is nothing short of perfection—a body that I have wanted to touch and taste for so long. I glance over at his bedside clock and see we have five minutes. Looking back at him, my gaze collides with his intense one as he stares down at me with undisguised hunger, and I feel a smile tug at my lips.

"Mmm, I always knew that mouth of yours was capable of the best things." Getting to my knees, I reach for the side zipper, underneath my arm, and unzip my dress. The straps slip down my shoulders and the silk falls away easily, leaving me completely bare. His eyes turn to liquid fire as he devours my naked body.

I crawl over top of the soft material until I'm directly in front of him and reach out tentatively to touch him. I'm a little worried that he won't let me, like last time, but he grabs my wrist and guides my hand to rest on his hard, defined abdomen. His gaze never wavers from mine as he leans down and claims my mouth. It isn't like any of the kisses we've had yet. It's not frantic and desperate; it's slow and deliberate. It sends warmth through my entire body and my heart into a tailspin.

When he pulls back, I take a minute before opening my eyes, wanting to bask in this moment as long as possible. When I eventually open them, I see him watching me with a small smile, and I can't help but return one of my own.

"You really can do wonders with that mouth of yours, McKay, and now I'm going to show you what mine is capable of."

Leaning down, I kiss his toned stomach before trailing my tongue along the contours of his abs. As much as I would like to take hours to explore every inch of his body, I know I don't have much time before he will have me on my back again, so I head right to the good stuff. I hook my thumbs on the inside of his waistband and pull his pants down just enough for his erection to spring free. I don't bother to finish ridding him of them before fisting his thick cock in my hand, loving the smooth, hard feel of it. He hisses out a breath and pumps himself into my firm grasp. When a pearl of clear fluid leaks from the tip, I lean in and lick it clean, loving the salty taste of him.

With a growl, he weaves his fingers in my hair and the firm grip stings my scalp in the best way. "Take me in, Kayla. All of me."

He doesn't need to tell me twice. Looking up at him with a smirk, I take him all the way in until he hits the back of my throat, then I suck back to the tip, making sure to run my tongue on the underside of it.

"Ah fuck, yeah. That's it, baby, suck my dick just like that."

I move to repeat the motion but he beats me to it and thrusts back in. A whimper escapes me and my clit flares to life again from his control. He sets the pace, which is hard and fast. I relax my throat and take him as far as I can and grip the base where my mouth can't reach.

He tugs my head back a bit so our gazes collide and keeps his pace, his eyes wild with lust. "You like it when I fuck this sassy mouth of yours, Kayla?"

I moan, letting him know that I love it, and I do. I usually don't like to be told what to do, but this guy can do anything he wants to me when our clothes are off. Hell, even with our clothes on I think I would do anything he says, which is a little scary.

"This is what I pictured doing to you every time you mouthed off to me. It drove me fucking crazy and you knew it."

Yes, I did. It's why I loved riling him up, because I knew one day he would make me pay for it in the dirtiest ways possible.

I feel him grow harder just before he pulls out of my mouth with lightning speed. "Why are you stopping?" I ask through labored breaths, my mouth watering for his taste.

"Because it's almost time and there is nothing in the world that will stop me from claiming what I have been waiting years to do." He leans down and pulls something from his pants pocket before putting a hand on my chest and coaxing me to lie down.

I scoot back a little closer to the headboard then watch him as he opens the condom and sheathes himself. His gaze is fierce as he crawls over top of me, his hard, bare body blanketing mine, sending a beautiful warmth flowing through me. I feel his erection on the inside of my thigh and my heart rate speeds up in anticipation. I'm not nervous though; I have wanted this for too damn long.

Cooper's expression softens as he reaches up and brushes a strand of hair out of my face. "There are so many ways I want to take you, so many things I want to do to you. But for now, I'm going to go slow and savor every minute of it, and I'll try to make it as painless as possible for you."

As much as I like his dominant side, I love this side of him too—his softer side. "It will be perfect because it's with you," I tell him truthfully.

He presses a kiss to my forehead then rises up on one arm and runs his erection through my wet flesh, coating it with my arousal. I moan when he grazes my sensitive clit. We both glance at the clock to see it's one minute after midnight.

"Kayla?" I look back at him to see a small smile on his face. "Happy birthday, baby." Then he enters me with one smooth thrust.

I gasp. The sting of pain is the most exquisite I've ever felt.

A deep groan erupts from his chest as he stills and gives me time to adjust. His back muscles are tight and strained under my fingertips.

"Shit. Just relax, baby." I relax my knees that have a strong grip on his hips and breathe through the fullness of him. "Better?" he asks a moment later.

"Yes."

Rising up, he begins thrusting inside of me with slow, deliberate strokes. It's tight, a little painful, and absolutely beautiful. "Jesus, you feel fucking incredible."

I reach up and frame his face between both of my hands, and pull him closer until his lips are only a breath from mine. As I stare into his warm, green eyes, I let it sink in that I am finally having the only man I've ever wanted. And now that I have him, I know that everything I have gone through, up until this point, was meant to lead me here—to this one person.

"What are you thinking?" he asks softly, as if sensing my thoughts.

I debate on how much to tell him then decide on the truth. "I'm pretty sure I've waited my whole life for this moment with you."

He falters and my heart thrums at a fast pace, scared that I just ruined the moment, but my fear vanishes when he gives me a small, genuine smile. "I have no doubt, Kayla, that you were made just for me." I feel the biggest, silliest smile take over my own face. "You and your sassy mouth that drives me fucking crazy."

"Mmm, you love my mouth," I throw back.

He grunts. "Now that I can do something with it I do."

A giggle escapes me, and we both groan when I clench around him. I feel his body begin to shake with restraint from holding back. Linking my arms around his neck, I hitch a leg up on his lower back, bringing him deeper. "Kiss me, McKay, then fuck me like you mean it."

With a growl, he claims my mouth then unwraps my arms from around his neck and pins them above my head. He pulls out so only the tip of him is inside of me then he slams back in. I gasp and arch up into him as tingles explode through my body.

"That okay?"

"God yes, keep going."

"My fucking pleasure." He pulls back again until he's almost out then slams back into me. He does this over and over, rocking my body with the best sensations. Our fingers link above my head and our bodies begin to stick from sweat. I finally find rhythm with him and thrust up into his beautiful, relentless assault. "That a girl, take me, Kayla, all of me."

I feel my tummy pull tight with my impending orgasm, and I begin to flutter around him.

He feels it and groans. "Yes, give it to me. Let me feel it, baby."

"Cooper?" I barely get his name out—I'm so enraptured in the moment—I'm not even certain of what I'm asking for. My fingers dig into his back as I feel my body teeter on the edge. I'm so close but can't grasp it.

"I got you." He changes the angle of his thrusts, hitting that spot deep inside of me at a hard, fast pace.

I can do nothing else but take it, and it feels incredible. "Oh god, oh god."

Unlinking one of his hands from mine, he moves it down to cup my breast and pinches my sensitive nipple with a force that has me detonating.

"Fuck yes!" Cooper increases his pace, faster than I thought possible, and fucks me through the intensity of my pleasure. I'm barely coming back down from my high when he stills deep inside of me and groans out his own pleasure.

We lie together in a sweat-tangled mess as we try to catch our breaths, our hearts beating together as one. I hold him as close as humanly possible, never wanting him to leave this spot inside of me. I feel his lips press gently against the corner of my forehead.

"You okay?" he asks, sounding a little concerned.

"Mmmhmmm," I hum, having a hard time forming words.

With a chuckle he pulls out of me, and we both groan at the disconnection. "I'll be right back."

Once he stands, I pull the blanket up to keep warm, since I no longer have his body heat, then enjoy the view as he walks to the bathroom. He comes back in his underwear a few minutes later, and begins to clean me with a warm washcloth. I tense at the awkwardness of it, but he puts me at ease when he presses a kiss to the inside of my thigh.

After he finishes, he throws it in his laundry hamper then crawls back in beside me and pulls me against him so we're face to face. We stare at each other for a long, silent moment and I can't help but smile. "Happy birthday to me."

He chuckles and presses a kiss to my forehead. "Yeah, baby. Happy birthday to you, and it's about fucking time."

I giggle and wrap my arms around his neck to bring him closer. "Mmm, agreed, and this was, by far, my favorite birthday gift ever."

His lips tilt with a mischievous smile. "That wasn't your birthday gift."

I quirk a brow. "No? You got something more for me, McKay?"

"Maybe," he replies secretively.

"It's handcuffs, isn't it? Let's put that shit to use right now."

He belts out a laugh and cups my ass in his big hands. "I don't need to buy you handcuffs. I get that shit for free."

I wait for him to say more but he doesn't. He only stares at me with a sly smile.

"Well, come on, give it to me already."

"Oh, I'll give it to you." With lightning speed he flips me to my back and comes over top of me, then kisses the living daylights out of me.

I sigh and decide I will never tire of him. Not ever. I distantly feel him reach over and hear the sound of a drawer being opened. Then before we can get caught up in our passion, he rolls off of me and leaves a small wrapped present on my chest.

I stare at it, wondering what it could be. "You didn't have to get me anything."

"I know, I wanted to. I've had it for a while."

I look over at him in surprise, my heart warming at that small tidbit of information. With giddy excitement I sit up, making sure the sheet is wrapped around me, and start opening it. My curiosity peeks at the small, velvet jewelry box. "You asking me to marry you already? I love it, Coop, but maybe we should wait until after graduation."

"Ha ha," he replies, deadpanned. "Just open it, smart-ass."

I open the box with a smile and falter when I get a look at the authentic, platinum Pandora charm bracelet. "Whoa," I whisper, not really knowing what else to say. I don't think there are any words to describe the beauty of this bracelet.

Cooper pulls it out of the box then takes my hand and puts it on my wrist. I start fingering the charms. The first one is a light pink heart. Next to it is the number three. "For three years." I glance over at him for confirmation, which he confirms with a nod. I touch the simple, deep blue charm beside it, trying to think of what it could mean, and he ends up answering my silent thought.

"For the color of your eyes."

I smile, my heart melting into a serious gigantic puddle. When I finger the next charm I burst into a fit of laughter at the small set of handcuffs. I look over at him to see a sly smile on his face. "Hmm, and you said you didn't get me handcuffs, you liar."

He gives me a sexy wink that has my heart flipping over in my chest. The sexy bastard. I glance down at the last charm and my head tilts in confusion as I study the ice cream cone, wondering what it could mean. I look over at him for the answer.

"There's actually a story behind that one," he says quietly then clears his throat, suddenly seeming nervous. "It's from the first time I saw you."

I frown at the charm, and remember the first time we ever met was when he moved in next door to me. "I didn't have an ice cream that day."

He watches me for a moment, and I wait for him to explain but what he says next is something I could have never expected. "I was pissed when my parents said we were moving back to my dad's hometown. I had it good where I lived before—star quarterback of the football team, lots of friends. I didn't want to come here and start all over. A few days before we moved, we were driving through town; my dad was taking us to see the house. It was a really hot day and I had my window down. We came to a stop at a red light when I suddenly heard some girl, yelling up a storm. I looked over to see what the ruckus was about and saw this beautiful blonde firecracker, who didn't look much younger than me, giving some guy shit for picking on another kid. They were in the parking lot of the ice cream shop and she was waving her pink ice cream cone all over the place. I actually thought she was going to throw it at the guy. When the asshole left and she turned around to help the kid up, the full view I got of her was like a punch to the chest. She was the prettiest girl I had ever laid eyes on. I hated it when that light turned green. I was tempted to jump out of my parents' car and run to meet this fiercely pissed off girl who looked like an angel but had the mouth of a sailor."

He pauses for only a brief second.

"Three days later we moved into the house. As I was carrying boxes, I felt someone's eyes on me. I looked up at the house next door and low and behold, the one girl I couldn't stop thinking about was staring down at me from her bedroom window. That day I realized that moving to this town wasn't going to be so bad after all, and it actually turned out to be the best thing that ever happened to me."

I gape at him in complete and utter shock, my vision blurry with unshed tears. I don't move, I can't. I am completely frozen in place, and I swear my heart literally stopped beating the moment he started his story. I remember that day at the ice cream parlor, when Jacob Larson was picking on Timmy Dickerhoff. He was even more mean than usual and pushed him down to look cool in front of his friend. Little did I know, that the guy I would become infatuated with saw me that day, waving my ice cream around like a lunatic.

When I don't say anything and continue to stare at him, Cooper reaches up and wipes my wet cheek before cupping it in his large hand. "That's why it killed me to think I made you feel like a bad person after our fight. Like you weren't good enough for me. That day I saw a girl who could have minded her own business but instead stopped to help someone and didn't care what anyone thought." Without taking his hand from my cheek, he sits up and moves in close, then drops his forehead on mine, his warm gaze penetrating. "The truth is, you're the best person I've ever known, Kayla, better than me. And I promise to make sure you always know it."

My breath hitches with emotion, and since I can't form any words at the moment, I crush my lips to his and kiss him for all I'm worth. My arms wrap tightly around his neck and he lies down, bringing me on top of him. Our mouths create a beautiful passion, my tears mixing in with the sweet taste we make together. I pull back a long moment later when my lungs desperately crave air but only slightly, making sure to keep our lips only a breath away from one another. I stare back into his warm, green eyes and try to think of the right thing to say, but there are no words to describe what I'm feeling. So with a small smile I decide to let him in on my future plans. "I'm going to marry you one day, Cooper McKay, so you better be ready for me."

He gives me his trademark sexy smile. "I'm never prepared when it comes to you, baby, but I wouldn't have it any other way."

With a giggle I attack his mouth again, but this time he flips me over and takes control. Just the way I like.

What started off being a terrible day turned out to be one of the best nights of my life…

I come back to the present and look around at all the girls who are sitting around me, hoping my face isn't as red as it feels when I think about what Coop did to me later that night. Obviously, I kept this story PG for Ruthie's sake.

"That is the most beautiful, real-life love story I've ever heard," Grace says with a hand over her heart.

I look down and finger the bracelet that is now loaded with charms; including the baseball bat to signify when I beat his truck after thinking he was cheating on me. I still feel like crap over it, but like Grams says, desperate times call for desperate measures.

"Well, I don't know about that, but it's my and Cooper's story, so it's perfect to me."

Just thinking about it has me craving to see him. We didn't sleep together last night since all of us girls stayed together. It's the first night we've been away from each other in, well, ever. I missed him like crazy, missed the safety of his arms and the feel of his hard, warm body wrapped protectively around me. Oh hell, I just missed every damn thing about him.

"God I'm so jealous," Katelyn says, almost sounding wistful. "Don't get me wrong, I'm happy for you all, but jealous as hell. You are all lucky to have found such amazing men who worship the ground you walk on."

"You will find your guy one day, Katelyn. I know it." Julia assures her with a soft smile.

"Not unless his name is Nick Stone." All of our eyes snap to Faith at her mumbled comment.

"Nick Stone? Who's Nick Stone, and why have I never heard of this guy?" I ask, my curiosity piquing at full intensity.

Katelyn glares over at Faith. "No one important. Just someone I used to know. He was one of Kolan's friends back in Montana."

I can tell he's a lot more than that, but there's no denying the flash of pain in her eyes as she talks about him, so I don't press. I don't know much about her past before coming here but I do know it wasn't pretty. Her brother, Kolan, is extremely protective over her. I've only met him a few times and he's really not all that friendly. I've also witnessed what he can do in the ring, and there is no denying the guy is lethal. Faith once told me he's very complicated. She said, other than her and Katelyn, he likes to keep to himself and ensures his life stays private. It surprised me considering he's in the media often for all of his fights. He's one of the best in the industry right now and is rising to the top fast.

Suddenly, Ruthie crawls over onto Katelyn's lap and slings an arm around her neck. "Don't worwy, Auntie Katewyn, you always have me, and I woship you."

All of us look at each other with a smile. Ruthie has the most beautiful heart of anyone I've ever known.

Katelyn's expression turns soft as she hugs her. "Thanks, sweetheart. I worship you, too."

Julia's phone dings with a text, interrupting the moment. She looks at it and gets the biggest smile. "Oh my god, you guys, look at Anna in her prom dress."

We all lean over to look at the picture of her and Logan. "They both look stunning," I say quietly.

"I sent her a picture of you already and told her I would send more as the night went on. She says you look beautiful."

I nod, hating that her prom fell on the same day as my wedding. She is a big part of our group and is important to us all, especially Julia and Jaxson. I wish she could have been here to celebrate with us, but I'm glad to see she's having a great time, if the smile on her face is anything to go by.

I glance back down at the pregnancy test and feel butterflies swirling around in my tummy again.

"Did you want to talk to Cooper before the wedding?" Julia asks. "I can go get him or text Jaxson to tell him to meet you somewhere."

I seriously consider it but quickly decide against it. There isn't much time before the ceremony, and I don't want him to see me before the wedding. I'm pretty sure he's going to be happy about the baby, like me, but I want to tell him when we have time to enjoy the news together. Not, *hey, babe, I just wanted to let you know that I'm pregnant. See ya down the aisle in a few minutes.*

I shake my head at Julia. "Nah. I'll tell him tonight after the ceremony. But can you pass me that empty gift bag there?" I ask, pointing to the bag that my garter came in. She passes it to me, and I put the test in then close it up. "Would someone mind taking this to our room for me?"

"I will," Katelyn says, standing. I give her my room key, once again thankful that we decided to have the entire wedding at the plantation for the sheer convenience of having it in one place.

Faith and Ruthie decide to go with her, and as soon as they open the door to leave, I hear my mom's voice. "Oh my gosh. Look at how stunning you girls are," she gushes. "Is my girl ready in there? Is everyone decent?"

I speak up before Katelyn can answer. "Yes, Mom, we're decent, you can come in."

She plows into the room and gasps when she sees me. "Oh my god, you look so beautiful," she blubbers and pulls me against her in a gripping hug.

I roll my eyes but can't deny the thickness I feel in my throat as I pat her back. "Thanks, Mom. You look beautiful, too."

Both her and Cooper's mom are wearing pink dresses too, but where my bridesmaid's dresses are silk, theirs are chiffon and a lighter tone of pink.

Suddenly, I catch sight of my dad as he walks in. "Whoa." He comes to an abrupt halt and puts a hand to his chest.

"Hey, Dad," I whisper, feeling my cheeks heat at his heart-stopping reaction.

After a long moment of staring at me, he walks over and pulls me into his arms. I breathe in deeply, taking in the safety and familiarity of his embrace. No matter how old I get, there is nothing more heart-warming than feeling my dad's arms around me. He was the first man I ever loved, and I'm so glad I found someone as amazing and honorable as him. "You're the most beautiful bride I've ever seen, next to your mother of course."

"Thank you." I feel him reach over and bring my mom into our hug then I hear a picture being snapped. Probably Julia.

"Isn't she beautiful?" my mom says, her voice laced with emotion. "Cooper isn't going to know what hit him."

I smile. Well, if my dress doesn't make his jaw drop, the baby news definitely will.

CHAPTER 7

Cooper

"I still can't believe she talked you into making us wear pink fucking ties. I swear my balls are shrinking by the second," Sawyer complains as he adjusts his tie in the mirror.

Yeah, well I don't like it either, but Kayla really wanted it and anything my girl wants I give her. Hell, I probably would have worn a pink fucking suit if it made her happy.

"Good," Jaxson says, clapping him on the back. "Now they will match your small dick."

All of us chuckle but Sawyer. "My dick is far from small, asshole. Just ask—"

A knock on the side door interrupts whatever arrogant remark was about to be made and opens to reveal Christopher. "Hey, some lady named Gladys out here is confused on what side she should sit on. I told her if she's friends with both of you she can pick anywhere, but she's insisting I ask you where you want her seated. She said she doesn't want to make Kayla jealous."

I groan and shake my head but everyone else seems to find it fucking hilarious. "Seat her on Kayla's side, next to Grams."

"Okay, I will, but I'll let Alissa deal with her. That old lady is grabby."

Don't I know it.

"Thanks, Christopher."

He nods then backs away, but before the door can close my mom comes barging in. "Oh my, look at how handsome all of you boys are." Strolling over, she grabs the lapels of my jacket then pulls me down and kisses my cheek. "I can't believe my baby boy is getting married today," she says with a quivering lip.

Oh jesus.

I'm just about to ask why she isn't with the girls but Evans walks over and grabs my face. "I know. I can't believe our baby is all grown up, pink ties and all."

I slap his hand away and shove him. "Get the fuck off of me."

"Cooper!" my mom gasps. "Don't talk to your friends like that or you won't have any at all."

I roll my eyes, but before I can respond Evans does. "Yeah, that really hurt my feelings, I might just up and leave you one man down."

I grunt. "You do that and I'll make sure to find the perfect guy to walk your Cupcake down the aisle."

His amusement vanishes in an instant and he points his finger at me. "That shit's not funny."

The rest of us chuckle, thinking it is.

"Okay, that's enough, boys, be nice to each other," my mom says as she starts adjusting my tie, her expression becoming somber. "I still can't believe your sister is missing your wedding."

"Mom, we've talked about this. She has a year left on her teaching contract then she will move here and we will see her all the time. I spoke with her this morning. It's all good, I promise."

She shakes her head, still not liking it, but I am fine with it. I've never been that close with my sister. I mean, she's awesome and all, but she's five years older than me and was in college when we moved to Sunset Bay. After getting her degree she travelled the world, teaching English abroad. She couldn't leave Korea to come today or else it would have been a breach in her contract. Kayla and I thought about waiting but I didn't want to, I've waited long enough. My sister and I are fine with it; my mom, however, is not.

"Aren't you supposed to be with the girls?" I ask, trying to bring her out of her thoughts.

"Yes, I'm on my way, but I wanted to quickly stop in and see my boys." She walks up to Jaxson and pulls him down for a hug. "You look as handsome as always. Julia and Annabelle are so lucky to have you."

Jaxson hugs her back easily, used to her affection. After his useless dad split on him, my parents insisted he live with us and they made him a part of the family. He's not only my best friend but also the closest person I have to a brother.

"Thanks, but I'm the lucky one."

My mom smiles at his response then walks over to my cousin Shawn next. "My favorite nephew. I'm so glad you could come and stand with Cooper on his special day."

I roll my eyes again. *Jesus, does she have to talk like we're fucking ten?*

"I'm your only nephew," he replies with a smirk.

"True, but you're still my favorite." She chuckles then moves on to Cade for a hug, which makes him uncomfortable but he's polite about it. The guy has gotten better, but if it isn't Faith or Ruthie he's still not all that comfortable with affection. Sawyer, of course, eats that shit up.

"All right, and one more for my boy before I go." She walks back over to me and wraps her arms around my waist. "I love you, and I'm so proud of you."

"Thanks, Mom," I mumble uncomfortably and want to punch Evans in the face at his smirk. Thankfully, my dad walks in and breaks up the awkward moment.

"Hey, Coach." Everyone greets him.

"How goes it, boys?" He shakes their hands and gives them a clap on the back. "All right, Arlene, let the boy go and head on over to the girls' suite. I just spoke with Pastor Williams and we're ready in five minutes."

"Okay, okay." She squeezes me one more time then looks up at me with a smile. "I'm excited to see Kayla, I know she's going to be beautiful today."

"She's beautiful every day." I answer honestly because it's the damn truth. No one, and I mean *no one*, holds a candle to her. She's the most beautiful girl in the world, inside and out. Even when she's a pain in the ass she's still sexy as hell, and fuck did I miss her sassy ass last night. I didn't sleep worth a shit without her and I never want to do that again. Not under any circumstance. I can't wait until the wedding is over so I can haul her ass upstairs to our room and show her how much I missed her.

"That certainly is true," my mother replies, snapping me from my thoughts. "Okay, I'm going now. Want me to give Kayla a message from you?"

I shake my head. The message I have for her is completely inappropriate for my mom to know.

"All right." She gives my father a kiss then waves one last time before walking out of the room.

My dad walks up to me now and claps me firmly on the back, like he did the others. "How are you doing? You nervous?"

I shake my head. "Nah, I'm ready."

That is a major understatement. I swear I was born ready for this moment.

My father nods. "Good. I promise not to get all mushy like your mom. Just know I'm proud of you too, kid."

"Thanks, Dad."

He pulls me in for a quick hug. "All right, let's go. Pastor Williams is waiting."

All of us head to the side door that leads to the outdoor garden where the ceremony is being held. Just as everyone walks out Jaxson holds me back. “Wait up a sec.”

I turn to him. He shifts nervously, and I quickly realize shit’s about to get uncomfortable again. “Listen, I just want to say…uh…” He rubs the back of his neck. “Fuck, I suck at this shit!”

“You’re not going to kiss me, are you?” I joke with a smirk, trying to lift the awkwardness of the moment.

He grunts then takes a moment as he finds his words. “I just want to say thanks…for everything. I owe a lot to you and your parents. If it hadn’t been for you, I probably wouldn’t have finished high school. You took care of Julia for me when I left, you beat the shit out of me when I needed it, and you’ve stuck with me through some of the worst moments of my life. You’re the brother I never had, and I guess I just…I wanted to say thank you. For all of it. And I’m glad I’m standing beside you today like you did me.”

I clap him on the shoulder. “You don’t need to thank me, you’ve done the same for me over the years. Although, you could have tried a little harder when my woman beat the fuck out of my truck that night, but hey…” I trail off with a shrug.

He grunts. “She threatened to bash my head in with that bat and we both know she would have.”

I chuckle. Yeah, I have no doubt she would have; she was pissed. It’s something I can joke about now but at the time it wasn’t funny. Not the damage to my truck, I didn’t care about that, but the fact that she thought I would cheat on her… I shake myself from the memory—the thought still bothers me.

Jaxson gives me a punch on the arm. “Come on, let’s get out there before you’re late for your own wedding.”

We head outside to see over two hundred friends and family seated on white, fancy chairs that have big fucking pink bows tied to them. I smile and nod at a few people as we walk down the aisle informally and take our spots next to Pastor Williams and the groomsmen. I turn to

Faith's father and clasp his hand. "Pastor, thank you again for being here with Kayla and me. We really appreciate it."

"You're welcome. I'm honored you guys asked me to be a part of it."

"Oh, Sheriff!" The old lady voice interrupts our greeting, and I look over nervously to where Gladys is sitting with Grams, waving at me with a coy smile.

I clear my throat awkwardly and give her a brief flick of my hand, which clearly is a mistake since she takes that as a sign to blow me a kiss.

"Damn, that lady is relentless," I mumble.

Jaxson slings an arm around my shoulders. "I told you, man, you need to stop going over there every time she tells you her panties have been stolen. You're leading the poor lady on." He chuckles.

I'm just about to tell him I do no such thing but the music begins playing, signaling it's time to start. I stand up straighter and watch both Kayla's mom and my mom take their seats up front. Kayla's mom waves and blows me a kiss then pulls some tissue out of her purse, taking one for herself then handing one to my mom.

Oh jesus, they are both going to be a blubbering mess the entire wedding. I know it.

Katelyn makes her way down the aisle first. I catch her make eye contact with my cousin, whom she will be walking back down with, and I look over to see him wink at her. When he looks at me, I give a subtle shake of my head, letting him know to back off. I warned him earlier to stay away from her. He's the biggest whore I know, and that girl has gone through enough shit, she doesn't need to deal with his, too.

Faith walks down next and blows a subtle kiss to Cade before taking her place beside Katelyn. Then it's Grace. She smiles shyly at Sawyer. I don't look over at his response, but whatever it is has her blushing furiously.

Go figure.

Julia follows in next, and I hear Jaxson exhale a breath. "I swear I'm the luckiest motherfucker alive."

"Yeah, you are," Sawyer adds, slightly above a whisper. "I still have no idea what she sees in you."

All of us chuckle under our breath, including Jaxson. Before Julia walks past me, she stops and kisses my cheek. "I can't wait for you to see her. She's perfect."

"She always is." I have no doubt that she looks incredible, but I've already seen her at her best. Naked, with me on top of her, inside of her, connected to her… *Oh shit.* I shift uncomfortably and pull myself from my thoughts before I get a boner in front of hundreds of people.

Julia steps back then turns to wait for Ruthie and Annabelle to make their way down. Ruthie holds Annabelle's hand as she walks slowly and unsteadily down the aisle. Everyone gushes and snaps a million pictures. Once they reach the end, Julia bends down and sweeps Annabelle up in her arms and kisses her cheek.

"You did so good, baby girl." She walks Annabelle over to Jaxson so he can kiss her too, then she takes her over to Grams's waiting arms.

Ruthie walks up to Cade before taking her spot next to the girls. "Wookin' good, Big Guy." All of us bite back a smile as she holds her fist out for a knuckle-bump.

"You too, kid. Always," he replies, knocking fists with her.

With a bright smile, she skips over to her spot and gives me a light punch in the arm as she passes by. "Goodwuck, Mister Shewiff."

"Thanks. Do you think I'm going to need it?"

"Well, she is hopin' to knock you on yowr ass."

We all burst into a fit of laughter, including Pastor Williams.

Faith leans down and pulls Ruthie in next to her. "Butt, honey, remember it's *butt* for you."

"Oh yeah, wight, sowwy."

Faith kisses her cheek, letting her know it's okay.

When the music changes and everyone stands, I swing my attention back to the aisle and suck in a sharp breath at the sight before me.

Ho-ly shit.

All the oxygen leaves my lungs as I stare awestruck at the girl whose arm is linked with her father's, as she walks toward me. I knew she would look amazing, but jesus…she looks like an angel, an innocent one, except I know she is anything but. I have corrupted her way too many times for her to be innocent any more. But as I take in her white, strapless dress, long blonde hair flowing down past her slender shoulders in big, loose curls and the veil high on her head—she looks like the most innocent angel that God has ever created. That's until her sweet, soft smile turns into something else the closer she gets. It's a smile that tells me she's up to something.

Stopping a short distance in front of me, her dad leans down and kisses her cheek. Just as he's about to pass me her hand, she pulls free and launches herself at me. I catch her in surprise with a grunted chuckle that quickly vanishes when she gives me one hot fucking kiss. I snap out of my shock quickly then take control, like always. A low growl escapes my throat as soon as her sweet taste touches my tongue, the deep sound is covered from everyone hooting and hollering at her unexpected act.

Kayla is the one to break the kiss first, and thank god she does because I probably would have never stopped. I keep hold of her, her feet still dangling off the ground and stare into her smiling face.

"I think the kiss comes at the end," I tell her with a smirk.

"I've never been one to follow the rules, Sheriff. You know that." She leans in closer then whispers, "But you can punish me for it later."

My amusement vanishes and I groan inwardly. "You can count on it. I have lost time to make up for. I missed you last night."

"Me, too," she replies softly.

I press a kiss to her forehead then drop her back on her feet.

"You like my dress?" she asks, giving me a little twirl.

Chuckles fill the air around us, including mine. "Yeah, baby." I pull her back in to me. "You look beautiful, just like always, but you're going to look even better when I take it off of you tonight."

"Mmmm, agreed." She reaches up and gives me another kiss, but this one ends much quicker than the last, much to my disappointment. Kayla steps back then looks up at Pastor Williams with a smile. "Sorry, Pastor, I just couldn't help myself. He looks so darn good in this suit of his."

She gives me a sassy wink that makes me want to haul her ass up to our room and say *fuck all this* and just sign the papers tomorrow. Somehow, I manage to restrain myself. It's what this woman does to me, what she has always done to me. She pushes every button I have with just a look, a wink, or a sassy remark—all to get a rise out of me. And she loves when I take it out on her later, when we are alone and—

"No problem. Whenever you're ready we can start," the pastor replies, interrupting my perverted thoughts.

"I'm ready," she says, then looks at me. "You ready?"

"I was born ready, baby."

She smiles. "Good answer."

With a chuckle the pastor starts, and thankfully the ceremony is fairly quick, which is what we wanted because South Carolina in June is hotter than hell. After the signing of the papers, exchange of rings, and vows, Pastor Williams finishes it with, "Now, by the power vested in me by the state of South Carolina, and as a minister of the gospel, I now pronounce you husband and wife. You may kiss—"

That's the last thing I catch before Kayla launches herself at me again. This time though, I'm prepared for her. I lift her off her feet once again and claim her mouth first. Our kiss is slower and more intimate than the last, and I get completely lost in her, like always. It doesn't matter how many times I've kissed this girl, I can never get enough of her.

She pulls back and drops her forehead on mine with a smile. "I told you I was going to marry you one day, Cooper McKay."

I return her smile with a smirk. "You did, but little did you know that was my plan long before yours."

With a sweet giggle, she leans in and kisses me again. "I love you, Officer Sexy," she mumbles against my lips.

"I love you too, baby."

CHAPTER 8

From the moment that kiss ended everything turned into chaos—from pictures in the smoldering heat, to supper, speeches, and now the first dance. I'm not a big dancer. Actually, I don't like it at all, but right now, as I hold Kayla's soft, slender body close to mine, I decide it's not such a bad thing after all. Even though we have hundreds of people watching us, I feel like, for the first time today, it's just her and me, and I'm thankful for the small reprieve.

"So, has it been everything you hoped it would be?" I ask.

She nods softly. "Yes, actually even more than I had hoped it would be." For some reason I get the feeling that her words hold meaning, but before I can think more of it, she reaches up and wraps her arms around my neck. "What about you?"

Most guys don't give a shit about things like this. I know girls think about this moment from the time they are kids, but us guys don't. Well, maybe the wedding night, but not the actual wedding. I couldn't have cared less what we did or where we had our wedding just as long as she was here. "Yeah, baby, because all I need is you."

"Well, yeah, it wouldn't have been anyone else or I would have cut a bitch."

I bust out laughing, knowing it's true. "I wish you would be more possessive where Gladys is concerned. Jesus, that lady has been relentless all night. Where are your ass kickin' skills when I need them?"

"Now come on, Coop, you don't really want me to kick an old lady's ass, do you? You should be flattered, Sheriff. I mean, she could call anyone to come find her panties, but she trusts your investigatin' skills to get the job done."

I grunt at her sarcasm, not finding it very funny, which only makes her laugh.

Unfortunately, that is not where my torment ends when it comes to Gladys. An hour later, when I'm sitting at a table with all the guys, she comes up to me, looking excited as shit because my wife just told her that I would dance with her. My eyes snap to Kayla on the dance floor, where she's dancing with the girls, and she gives me a sassy little wave of her fingers.

Oh, she is going to fucking pay for this.

I look back up at Gladys's hopeful expression and try to figure out how the fuck I'm going to get out of this. "Well, that's real nice of you, Miss Gladys, but unfortunately, I'm not a very good dancer." Her face falls, making me feel like shit, so I add, "But Sawyer here loves to dance."

Her face lights back up, and I feel Sawyer's hard gaze on me, but I don't acknowledge him. That will teach the fucker for messing with me about the pink ties.

"Oh, he will work just fine, too." She turns to Sawyer. "What's your favorite dance, sugar?"

Jaxson chuckles next to me, and when I glance over at Sawyer, I swear if looks could kill I would be ten feet under right now. He snaps out of it quickly and pastes a smile on his face. "Sorry, but I'm only allowed to dance with my Cupcake. She gets really mad if I dance with other women, especially ones as beautiful as you, and I sure wouldn't want to hurt her feelings."

What a smooth motherfucker.

Gladys nods, as if fully understanding this. "Oh yes, I get that a lot. It seems the younger ladies do find me a little threatening, and I love Miss Grace. I wouldn't want her feelings hurt either."

You have got to be shittin' me.

I start feeling like an ass as she watches us eagerly, waiting for one of us to fill the role. Right when I think I'm fucked and have no other choice but to dance with her, old Gus, Kayla's grandpa, comes walking over and asks her. She's caught off guard but happily accepts then walks off arm in arm with him.

Thank fuck!

I glance back to Kayla to see her looking amused as shit. When she gives me a wink, I shake my head to let her know she's going to pay for this later. Suddenly, a napkin gets thrown at me from across the table and pulls me from our stare down.

"You fucker!" Sawyer berates me under his breath. "Why the hell did you throw me under the bus? Why not him?" He points to Jaxson.

I whip the napkin back at him. "Because he hasn't been annoying me by running his mouth all day about the pink fucking ties."

He grunts. "That's because he enjoys dressing like a chick, too." Jaxson throws his napkin at him now, which he catches with a laugh. "Oh calm your shit, ladies, I'm kidding. And what the hell are you thinking inviting that lady anyway? I mean, jesus, she is off her fucking rocker and you know it."

"Yeah, but she's harmless…most of the time, and Kayla said we had to since she's Grams's friend."

It's pretty much the only reason I agreed to it.

Before anyone can say more, Ruthie comes skipping over and jumps up on Cade's lap. Her beanie is now back on her head, even though she's still in her flower girl dress, but I have to admit, if anyone can pull it off it's her. "Hey, Big Guy, you havin' fun?" she asks Cade.

"Yeah. How about you?"

"Oh yes. I tan't wait until you and Faif get married, and I weally tan't wait to be your best man, or I guess I should say best girl," she adds with a giggle.

He smirks. "Me too, kid."

Cade and Faith's wedding is in a few months. Sawyer was always his best man while Jaxson, Christopher, and I are his groomsmen. Then Ruthie told him that the best man is supposed to be his best friend, and since she's his best friend she asked if she could stand next to him. Of course he said yes. Who could say no to her? However, we have all agreed that Sawyer is still in charge of the bachelor party.

The conversation gets broken up when the music suddenly switches from a slow song to a fast one, "I'm Sexy and I Know It", blaring loudly from the speakers.

"Oh my gosh, Sawyer." Grace squeals from across the dance floor, drawing all of our attention. "It's your song," she yells with a laugh then turns to him and starts dancing along. When she kisses each of her biceps we all burst into a fit of laughter.

Sawyer isn't fazed in the least—he's too arrogant. Instead, he watches her with an amused smirk then gets up and makes his way to the dance floor. We all groan because we know what's coming and so does Grace, if her attempt to dodge him is any indication. Of course she isn't able to make her escape. Bending down, he picks her up, sweeping her off her feet.

"Put me down, Sawyer!" she demands with a laugh.

"Sorry, Cupcake, but no can do. We have some business to take care of."

We all shake our heads as he walks out of the tent.

"Where's he takin' her?" Ruthie asks.

"Nowhere!" All of us shout at once.

I hope wherever he's taking her, he has the decency to go somewhere private, or better yet their room.

Ruthie lets out a big yawn and drops her head on Cade's chest, her eyes getting droopy. "You tired, kid? Want Christopher and Alissa to take you to bed?"

"No, I'm okay," she replies sleepily, then passes out not even two minutes later. Christopher and Alissa carry her to the suite Cade and Faith rented, and take Annabelle with them also.

Sawyer and Grace return thirty minutes later, Sawyer looking cocky and Grace looking…well, satisfied but clearly embarrassed, if her red cheeks and lack of eye contact with any of us guys is anything to go by.

At the very end of the night, after everyone has cleared out and the staff is cleaning up, all of us friends walk out to the garden for one last drink. Katelyn headed up to her room a little while ago, while my cousin left with some chick Kayla works with. Us guys are sitting on the stone steps to the fountain while the girls sit on our laps and talk about the day's events.

"It really was an amazing day. Thank you for letting us be a part of it," Faith says, and a chorus of agreement goes around.

"No, thank you, all of you," Kayla speaks for the both of us. "We couldn't have asked for a better wedding party. Coop and I are very thankful for you guys… Even you, Hulk," she adds, glancing over at Jaxson. "And to think, you didn't turn green once today, I'm so damn proud of you."

He grunts at her smart mouth. "I guess we both deserve a pat on the back then, because just think—you didn't take a bat to anyone's truck tonight."

She punches him in the arm. "Well, the night's not over yet. Where did you park again?"

All of us chuckle at their usual bantering.

"We definitely have been through a lot together," Julia says softly, steering the conversation back to the original topic. "I tell Jaxson all the time how blessed we are to have each other. We're more than friends, we're family, and I know our kids will grow up to be close, too."

Sawyer points at me with a smirk. "I guess it's time for you to get cracking on your baby-making skills, Sheriff."

I grunt. "Not yet."

Kayla tenses on me, but before I can think too much of it, the shrill ringing of a cell phone sounds. With a confused frown, Jaxson pulls his phone out of his pocket and glances at the number before answering. "Anna?" His expression immediately puts me on alert. "Whoa, calm down. I can't understand anything you're saying. Just take a deep breath." He puts a finger to his ear, trying to hear her better.

All of us look at each other, as we can hear a hysterical Anna on the other end of the line but can't make out what she's saying.

"What! What do you mean? How… Okay, okay, calm down. Just sit tight. I'm on my way." Jaxson hangs up and stands up quickly, lifting Julia to her feet.

"Jax, what's going on?" she asks in concern.

"That was Anna. She's at the police station." He pauses and looks at all of us, his expression unreadable. "Logan has been arrested for murder."

"What!" We all shout at the same time.

"I don't know what happened, she was so hysterical that I could barely understand her, but she wants me to come there." He looks at Julia. "I told her I would come. Can you go get Annabelle? Then we'll go home and pack a bag."

"Jax, that might take too long, and she's sleeping. Why don't you go tonight and Annabelle and I will come tomorrow?"

He shakes his head. "No. I don't want to leave you two, and I don't want you driving yourself there."

"Grace and I will stay with her," Sawyer offers. "I can drive them up tomorrow if you're still there."

"You sure?"

Instead of repeating himself, he replies with a nod. Jaxson is still reluctant but Julia convinces him it's for the best.

"All right." He leans down and kisses her. "I'll see you tomorrow, baby."

"Drive carefully," she says softly. "Text me when you get there and tell Anna I love her."

He nods then glances at me but I wave him away. "Go, just call me tomorrow and fill me in on what's going on. You know I'll help any way I can."

"Thanks." After a quick good-bye to everyone else he's gone.

We all get up to head to our rooms now, everyone silent while we ponder what could have happened. It's clear Logan has been through some shit, but I would never peg him for killing someone in cold blood. I shake my head. No, he wouldn't. I've gotten to know him well enough over the last two years, and I know he wouldn't do that. Something else is going on.

After one last good-bye to the others, Kayla and I walk to our room that's on the opposite side of the house. Closing the door behind me, I turn to see her standing in the middle of the room, looking tired and upset. I walk over and pull her in my arms. "You okay, baby?"

"Yeah, I'm just worried about Anna and Logan. I hope they're okay."

"They will be. Jaxson will make sure of it."

She looks up at me with a soft smile and nods. "Yeah, you're right."

I cup the side of her face and brush my thumb across her lush bottom lip. She turns her face to the side and kisses my palm. Just as I lean down to claim her mouth, she slaps a hand over my lips, stopping my attempt. "Hold it right there, Officer Sexy. Keep that delicious mouth away for just a moment. I have something that I need to tell you first."

I ignore her protest and pull her hand away. "We can talk later, baby."

She shakes her head. "No, we can't. It's important, Cooper."

I immediately back off at her underlying tone. "What's wrong?"

"Nothing is wrong, per se." She bites her thumbnail nervously, taking my concern to a whole new level.

"Kayla…"

"Can I ask you something?"

The vulnerability in her voice is starting to scare the shit out of me. "Always, baby, you know that."

She clears her throat and nods. "What did you mean down there when Sawyer said it was time for us to make a baby and you said 'not yet'?"

I rear back, caught off guard by the question and the fact that she seems upset by it. "I didn't mean anything. We talked about starting a family in a year or so and you just went off the pill—"

"Well, sometimes things change."

My brow furrows at her quiet reply. "Yeah, I guess it can." I shrug, still trying to figure out where this is all coming from. "Where are you going with this, Kayla?"

Her gaze focuses to something behind me, then she heads over to the antique dresser and grabs a small, silver gift bag off the top of it. She walks back up to me warily and hands it to me. "Here, open it. It's uh, it's kind of my wedding gift to you."

Oh shit!

"We're supposed to get each other gifts? I didn't know that."

She smiles at my sudden panic. "No, we aren't supposed to, but this was a surprise present for me this morning and now I'm gifting it to you."

Okay, now I'm completely intrigued. Taking a seat at the end of the bed, I open the bag and pull out a white stick that has a blue plus sign in the window. I tense and my eyes shoot to Kayla to see her watching me nervously. "What's this?" I ask, even though I know exactly what it is.

"A pregnancy test… *My* pregnancy test."

"You're pregnant?" I ask in shock.

She nods. "I found out this morning. I wanted to tell you earlier, but I thought it was best to wait until we were alone so we could talk about it."

I glance back down at the test and try to let it sink in that we're going to have a baby. I guess I shouldn't be surprised, considering she went off the pill, but the doctor said it could take up to a year to conceive.

"Say something," she whispers, her voice thick with worry.

I look back up at her and my chest constricts at her expression. "Jesus, Kayla." Reaching out, I grab her wrist and pull her to stand between my legs. "Why are you so nervous about my reaction? You have to know I'm not upset about this."

She expels a relieved breath then shrugs. "Well, I didn't think you would be, but then downstairs you said that to Sawyer, and I—I got worried." She shakes her head. "I don't know. I'm being stupid, I'm sorry."

"No, I'm sorry. I didn't mean anything by it. I'm happy, baby. Surprised as hell, but…really happy."

And a little fucking scared, but I decide to keep that part to myself.

I'm not scared for the responsibility, I'm more so worried about bringing a life into a world that can be very ugly at times. It's something I see on a regular basis. The thought of something happening to anyone I care about scares me, but the thought of it happening to Kayla or our future family is completely fucking terrifying.

Wrapping my arms around her waist, I drop my forehead to her stomach. "I promise I'll take really good care of our family, Kayla. I'll always protect you guys."

Her slender fingers thread through my hair as she holds me close. "I never doubted that for one second. I know you will take good care of us like you do everyone else in this town."

I glance back up at her. "Yeah, but you will always be my first priority. You know that, right?" I mean that with everything I am. My job means a lot to me and I will always uphold it, but my family will always come first—she will always come first.

"Yeah, Coop, I know that. I have no doubt you're going to be the best father our kids can ever have." Suddenly, a smile graces her lips. "Let's just hope they are like you and nothing like me, or you're in some serious trouble."

The thought of having a bunch of sassy little Kaylas running around does kind of scare the shit out of me.

She senses my thoughts and bursts out laughing. "I love your silence."

"Sorry," I apologize with a smirk. "But the thought is a little terrifying. My hands are full enough with just one of you."

"Mmm, don't be sorry." She backs out of my arms with a saucy smile. "I like it when your hands are full of me." My dick comes roaring to life as I watch her reach behind her back to undo her dress. I begin to stand up but she shakes her head. "Uh-uh, stay there. I have something to show you."

I already know exactly what she has under there; just the thought of it has fire pumping through my blood. But I sit back down then rid myself of my jacket, shirt, and tie, making sure my eyes never leave her body. My cock twitches at her blatant eye-fuck of my shirtless state. She takes her time ridding herself of the dress, trying to give me a show, but I'm way too impatient for that right now.

"Kayla, hurry the fuck up before I rip that thing off of you myself."

"Mmmm, a little impatient are we, Sheriff?" She mouths back, jacking my dick up another notch.

"Yeah, baby, I'm always impatient for your pussy." Undoing my pants, I free myself then take my cock into my hand with a firm grip. She freezes and her eyes glaze over with lust as she watches me stroke myself. A low groan rumbles deep in my throat. "Drop the dress, Kayla, now."

She quickly follows my order and I inhale a swift, sharp breath at what she reveals—her tight, fuckable body encased in a strapless, white lace bra and matching panties that are attached to a garter belt and stockings. My eyes sweep down the length of her, taking in her perfection. Her veil still drapes down her hair, and once again she looks angelic and innocent when I know she's really a vixen.

"I kept it simple so it wouldn't take you too long to get it off of me."

My gaze snaps back to her face to see a brazen smile tilting her lips. "Come here," I demand gruffly. She does as I tell her and comes to stand between my legs. I release my cock then cup her firm, round ass and groan when I realize she's wearing a thong. Leaning in, I press a kiss to her soft, toned stomach. "Do you have any idea how hard it makes me to know my baby is growing inside of this beautiful body of yours?"

I feel her shiver at my breath on her skin. "No, but I'm glad to hear it, because this body is going to be making some changes over the next nine months. And you better still find my ass sexy, because I have no plans to stop jumping your bones every chance I get."

I chuckle but it trails off on a groan when I think about all the times she surprises me at work because she doesn't want to wait until I get home. Those are always the best fucking days.

"Believe me, baby, you're going to be even more beautiful, if that's possible." I circle her naval with my tongue, loving the taste of her skin. "Know why?"

"No, why?" she whispers as her hands find my shoulders to keep balance.

"Because no matter where you are, what you're doing, or who you're with, there will always be a part of me inside of you, and there is nothing fucking hotter than that."

"Mmmm, well when you put it like that, that's downright beautiful."

"Yeah, baby, you're beautiful, always." I trail my lips lower, bringing them to the center of her panties, then skim my nose along the damp lace and breathe in deeply. Her sweet aroma penetrates my senses and my mouth instantly waters for a taste of her.

"Cooper." She moans while her fingernails bite into my shoulders.

"What do you want, Kayla, hmmm?" I hum against her. "You want my tongue buried deep in this sweet pussy of yours."

"God, yes." She whimpers and thrusts against my mouth.

My hand moves behind one of her knees and I lift it up to prop her foot on the bed, next to me, opening her up more to my view. She reaches up to take off her veil but I grab her wrist and stop her. "Leave it on."

She quirks a brow. "Whatever you say, Sheriff."

Leaning in, I nip the inside of her thigh just above where her stocking ends and watch goose bumps break out over her soft, delicate skin. She inhales sharply and her breathing turns ragged. I glance up at her just before I rip the garter belt and panties from her body with one swift pull. Her gasp trails off into a moan, and I grip her hips when she loses her balance.

A low growl erupts from me when I take in her slick, bare folds that glisten with her arousal. "Such a pretty pussy," I murmur. "And it's all mine, isn't that right?"

"Yes, yours, always." Her voice drops to a whisper.

"That's right, for fucking ever, until death do us part." I spread her open with my fingers and blow gently on her clit. Her knees buckle, but I quickly grab her ass to hold her up.

"Oh god, please, Cooper," she pleads on a moan, bringing my restraint to its breaking point.

"Please what?" I ask, glancing up at her again.

She stares down at me with her cheeks flushed and eyes glazed with naked lust, knowing exactly what I want to hear. She licks her lips, making my cock jerk at the sight of it. “Please lick my pussy.”

I groan at her soft words. “My fucking pleasure.” Leaning in, I take a long, leisurely lick of her warm, wet flesh and growl as her flavor explodes on my tongue.

“Ah yes!” she cries out. Her stance weakens again, but I cup her ass tighter to keep her from falling. I hear something drop to the floor and look up to see she rid herself of her bra, her perfect tits filling her hands. The sight of her is almost enough to make me come.

Her hips start rocking at a frantic pace as I devour her. “That a girl, fuck my mouth.”

“Oh god. It feels so good,” she confesses with a whimper. I feel her clit start to swell so I bring my hand up behind her and drag two fingers along the crevice of her ass before slamming them deep inside of her. “Ahhh!” As soon as her inner walls lock down on me, I catch her fluttering bud between my lips and send her over the edge. Her fingers grip my hair and her head falls back on a cry as ecstasy washes over her face. I don’t let up until every ounce of pleasure has spilled from her.

She drops down and straddles me, her stocking-covered thighs on either side of my hips. Her arms wrap around my neck and our mouths meet frantically. I thread my hand through her thick, curly locks, and pull her head back to deepen the kiss.

Unable to withstand not being inside of her for another second, I shove my pants further down my legs and slip inside of her tight heat without breaking contact with her mouth.

“Ah, fuck you’re perfect.” I groan as heat explodes through my entire body, her pussy gripping me like a tight vise. I swear there is nothing in the world that is better than being inside of this girl. I have been fucking her for years and every time I enter her it feels like the first time.

“I love you so much,” she whispers against my mouth.

"I love you, too, baby. Forever."

"Yes, forever."

Damn fucking straight. I will never tire of her—not her smile, her body, or her sassy mouth. Not even a lifetime with her will be enough.

Bringing my hand up, I cup the heavy weight of one of her firm, round tits and brush my thumb over the hard tip. Her head falls back in pleasure and she arches into my touch, giving me the perfect opportunity to lean in and take her other nipple into my mouth.

"Oh god, yes." Her fingers wind in my hair with a painful grip that shoots straight to my cock and her hips pick up rhythm.

"That's right, baby, fuck me." I lean back on my arms to bring her deeper, then slam up inside of her. All the breath leaves her lungs and she falls forward, bracing her hands on my stomach.

"Yes, again!"

I groan. "You want it hard and fast, Kayla?"

"Yes! I want it all."

With a growl, I grip her hips and start fucking her with an urgency that makes me feel like an animal, pounding up into her relentlessly. Pleasured cries spill past her lips as she claws at my chest to hang on, her nails marking me while her tits bounce enticingly in my face. Feeling close to exploding already, I change the angle of my thrusts and hit her sweet spot. Her pussy starts to flutter around me, warning me of her impending orgasm.

"That's it, give me another one, baby. Let me feel this pussy milk my cock."

I reach up and deliver a light slap to her tit, right over her beaded nipple, and it was all she needed. Her inner walls clamp down on me and send me over the edge with her. Ecstasy rushes through my veins as I continue my pace, fucking her hard and fast through our orgasms.

When we're both spent, she drops down on top of me, our sweat-slicked bodies molding together. I wrap my arms tightly around her and hold her close as we catch our breaths, our hearts pounding against one another. I drag my fingers along her back as we lie in comfortable silence—no words needed.

A few minutes later, I kiss the top of her head. "Come on, baby, let's shower before we fall asleep." Just as I sit us up, a big bang has me struggling to maintain balance to stop us from rolling off the bed.

Kayla gasps. "Oh shit! Did we break the bed?" She jumps off and looks underneath it then glances back up at me in horror. "Oh my god, we did! We broke the bed!"

"What? What kind of bed can't withstand a good fuck?"

A long bout of silence stretches between us before we both burst out laughing. "Damn it! They are going to charge us a fortune for this, I know it." Her voice has an edge of worry to it as she rips her veil off her head.

"At least it was money well spent."

She laughs again like I hoped for her to.

Bending down, I scoop her up in my arms then walk to the bathroom. "Don't worry, baby, we'll figure it out."

"Speak for yourself, buddy. I'm bailing early in the morning and totally blaming the whole thing on you."

I grunt, not putting it past her.

We shower and dry off quickly, both of us exhausted from the day's events. When we walk back out to the room, I use a phone book to prop up the broken side of the bed, making it close to level. Then I crawl in next to Kayla and pull her warm, naked body against mine. She looks up at me, her expression unreadable.

"We're married," she whispers, her tone serious.

"Yeah…" I reply slowly and stare down at her, unsure of where she's going with this.

"That means I'm your wife. Forever. Until you die." Her head tilts and her eyes turn crazy. "You are mine and there is no escape for you,

Cooper. Do you understand? If you ever try to leave me, I will find you, and I will kill you!"

I roll my eyes at her dramatics and lay a hand over her face, covering up her crazy-ass expression. "Thanks for the warning, Black Widow, but I don't plan on going anywhere. I like my new truck too much," I add with a smirk.

She laughs and slaps my hand away from her face. I keep hold of her hand and twine our fingers together to see how our rings look next to each other. "Do you feel different?" she asks quietly.

"What do you mean?"

"I don't know. We're married now and just found out we're having a baby; shouldn't we feel different?"

I shrug. "I don't see why. We always knew our lives were headed in this direction, and I love you the same as I did yesterday."

"Shouldn't you love me more every day?" she teases, quirking a brow at me.

"That's impossible, because I've loved you with everything I have from the day I made you mine, and I will for the rest of my life. Nothing—or no one—will ever change that, Kayla," I tell her truthfully.

She smiles softly; it's one of those smiles that constricts my chest and makes it difficult to breathe. "You always know the right thing to say to me." She leans in and places a kiss over my heart. "I'll never stop loving you either."

"Damn straight, or I will find you, and I will kill you," I mock back the teasing threat to her.

She giggles and we fall back into a comfortable silence again.

A few minutes later my eyes begin to feel heavy but I force them to stay open, wanting to say one last thing to her. "Kayla?" I whisper, not wanting to wake her if she's already fallen asleep.

"Yeah?" she replies just as quietly.

I reach down and place my hand flat against her stomach. "What I said earlier about the baby… I lied." She stiffens, but before she can say anything, I continue, "I hope all of our kids turn out just like you—kind, brave, generous, and a pain in the ass."

I feel her smile against my chest before she reaches down and places her hand over mine. "We're going to have a good life, Coop."

"Yeah, we are." Leaning down, I kiss the top of her head. "Sleep, baby." Are the last words I speak before I fall into a deep slumber.

Kayla

I hear Cooper's breathing even out and his hand gets heavier on my tummy. Looking up, I see his handsome face soft with sleep, and I watch him for a moment, taking in his unguarded expression like I do on so many nights. This is also one of my favorite moments in life that I cherish—to watch him when the world isn't weighing so heavily on him, as he shoulders so much responsibility. What he doesn't know, is that while he's watching over everyone and taking care of everything, I'm watching out for him and I always will. I know there will be times throughout our life that won't always be easy, but I will never give up on us—never give up on him. He was the first man I ever loved and he will be my last. I will make sure that we share as many unforgettable moments as possible, ones that will stay with us to eternity.

THE END

Turn the page for the prologue to *An Act of Redemption*. Book one in the *Acts of Honor series,* Logan and Anna's story, available now.

PROLOGUE

Anna

When I was fourteen years old I was abducted into the sex trafficking industry while on a field trip with my school in Thailand. It was the worst week of my life. I lost my best friend, Maddie, and had my innocence stolen from me. I didn't think I would come out of it alive, but thanks to Jaxson Reid, who I now consider my big brother, and two other brave Navy SEALs, I survived. A little damaged but alive. I wasn't sure I would ever be able to overcome what happened to me, but I did, and I came out stronger. I'd like to say it was from the extensive group therapy I did along with the support of my parents, and although I know that helped, it was actually all because of one person—Logan Knight. A guy who was misunderstood by most people and perceived as dangerous, but I've always known better. I saw in him what no one else did and we formed a connection, one that, even with a break in time, could never be severed.

In the beginning he was my salvation, but in the end I was his redemption.

This is our story.

Acknowledgements

I always have so many people to thank who help me through this amazing journey I am on. Let's hope I don't miss anyone.

Always first on my list is my amazing and incredibly supportive husband~ I feel like a broken record because it's always the same, but thank you. Thank you for loving me, for supporting me, and most of all, for making my dreams come true. You're the best husband in the world and an even better father to our beautiful children. It's clear I am a romantic at heart, and although I love all the love stories I write, ours is my favorite.

To my editor, Megan~ I have two words for you, BOOK FIVE! Okay, I'm lying, I have a few more for you. I don't think I will ever be able to say thank you enough. Not only for being an amazing friend but also editor. I know we don't always see eye to eye and you probably want to slap me sometimes, lol, but I want to say thank you for always bearing with me. When we are close to the end and I'm stressed or second-guessing myself, you are patient and always build me back up. That means more to me than you will ever know. So, again, thank you for continuing this amazing journey with me.

My parents~ Dad, I know you will never read any of my books and that is more than okay with me, because in the end I know you're proud of me. And we both know I'm your favorite child, sooo... ;) Mom, where do I start with you? I am pretty sure you have more friends in this indie world than I do, but what they don't have is you as their mom. I am not sure if they are lucky or not. Lol! I'm kidding, Karebear, I love you. Thank you for always being there for me and being my number one fan. Your love and support means everything to me.

My mother-in-law, Gis- I've said it before but I can never say it enough. Thank you for stepping out of your comfort zone by reading my books, and for still loving me afterward. Lol! Thank you for always being the first person to offer a helping hand with my beautiful children so I can be successful in this journey I'm on. You will never know how much it means to me to know my kids are in good hands when I'm gone and needed elsewhere. I also want to say thank you for raising such an amazing son. I have both you and Les to thank for me having my HEA (Happily Ever After).

Shelley- Thank you for always being an extra set of sharp eyes and for always having my back. Love you.

My betas – Kim, Sian, and Natasha- Thank you ladies for never steering me wrong, and for listening to me vent when I need to. I always appreciate you ladies being there for me and lifting me up.

Steph- My sister from another mister, I love you so much. Thanks for always being there for me in this crazy indie world. I can't wait for *Kingston*.

Keisha, aka K. Langston, aka one of my favorite authors, aka my new author bestie- I am so happy that not only do I now read your books, but that I also know you as a person. You always inspired me to be a better writer, but since knowing you, you also inspire me to be a better person. I love you, Hooker, thanks for showing me what it's all about.

My Cupcakes- You all mean more to me than you will ever know. I say it all the time and I will say it again—you girls are one of the best things that ever happened to me in this indie world. Thank you for your unwavering support. I couldn't do this without any of you.

Sian- Girl, you are a pimping queen. Thank you so much for always taking time out of your day to share my books. Your love and support completely overwhelm me in the best way. I can't wait to give you a squeeze in Ireland next year.

Sierra and Kim~ Thank you, ladies, for always being there for me when I need to vent, for coming to any of my signings when you can to support me, and for always having my back. Both of you started as readers and have become my besties. Love you to pieces.

To all my author buddies~ I am scared to name any of you and forget someone, but you know who you are. Lol! Thank you for always supportive and encouraging me. This indie world can get cray cray at times and it's nice to know you aren't alone and we have each other's back.

Bloggers, this is for you~

B~ Believe in us

L~ Lift us

O~ Open their hearts to us

G~ Go above and beyond

G~ Give us strength

E~ Encourage us

R~ Review and Recommend us

S~ Spread the love

To all the bloggers who love and support~ Thank you from the bottom of my heart.

Kari Ayasha~ Thank you for a beautiful cover, as always. I can always count on you to deliver exceptional work.

And last, but certainly not least, my Ladies Of Honor~ Your continued support is amazing and it's the love that you all constantly show me that keeps my head high and my fingers typing. Thank you and I love you all.

Author Bio

K.C. Lynn is a small town girl living in Western Canada. She grew up in a family of four children—two sisters and a brother. Her mother was the lady who baked homemade goods for everyone on the street and her father was a respected man who worked in the RCMP. He's since retired and now works for the criminal justice system. This being one of the things that inspires K.C. to write romantic suspense about the trials and triumphs of our heroes.

K.C. married her high school sweetheart and they started a big family of their own—two adorable girls and a set of handsome twin boys. They still reside in the same small town but K.C.'s heart has always longed for the south, where everyone says 'y'all' and eats biscuits and gravy for breakfast.

It was her love for romance books that gave K.C. the courage to sit down and write her own novel. It was then a beautiful world opened up and she found what she was meant to do…write.

When K.C.'s not spending time with her beautiful family, she can be found in her writing cave, living in the fabulous minds of her characters and their stories.

Printed in Great Britain
by Amazon